LIFE IN THE FRENCH QUARTER

A Novel

~~~~~~~~~~~~~~~~~~~~~~~~~

Andrea Lynn Biundo

For more information about the book or the French Quarter, go to www.LifeInTheFrenchQuarter.com

Cover art by JK Schwehm
www.figstreet.com

This is a work of fiction.

ISBN 978-0-9818745-2-4

Life in the French Quarter by Andrea Lynn Biundo

2nd Edition. June 2010

Published in the United States by Olbia Press

This book is dedicated to the beautiful city of New Orleans and all who have loved her.

"Instinct . . . directed me here, to the Vieux Carré

of New Orleans . . . I couldn't have consciously,

deliberately selected a better place than here to

discover—to encounter—my true nature."

~ Tennessee Williams (from his play Vieux Carré)

Contents

Prologue

When I first arrived in New Orleans, I felt as if a part of me had always been there. Sometimes a place just fits you perfectly, at least for a certain time period in your life.

I got a job at a blues club on Bourbon Street. That's where the French Quarter really began for me. If I had never gone in there, my experiences would have been entirely different, and I probably wouldn't have stayed in the Quarter as long as I did. I certainly didn't intend to.

A lot of people do that: They go to New Orleans for Super Bowl or Mardi Gras or Jazz Fest or whatever, but when it comes time to leave, they don't. They get caught up in the lights, the sounds, the smells, the flavors, and they stay. That's what happened to me when I walked into that blues club—that was my spider web. That's where all my entanglements began.

Allegedly, it was the former stomping grounds of Mark Twain, Jean and Pierre Lafitte, Walt Whitman, and a bunch of other famous dead guys. I walked the same streets, leaned against some of the same walls, and possibly even breathed in some of the same dust that they had. I never saw any ghosts, but I had some strange dreams, and I met a lot of interesting people.

If the bricks and cobwebs in the French Quarter could talk, they'd have a lot of stories to tell, I'm sure. Mine is just one.

1
First Few Weeks in the Quarter

As the plane circled down over New Orleans, I had the overwhelming feeling that I was going home. Not home in any kind of obligatory sense—of going to see people because you're supposed to or even because you want to. But home as in a sense of place, a place where you belong, regardless of people or buildings or anything man-made . . . as if the very dirt itself is calling your name.

Yes, I was running away, but it felt more like running away *to* the place I belonged, rather than just running away from the place where I didn't.

New Orleans was not the city I'd been born in, but it was my adopted home, and I was returning. Not uptown this time, I was moving into the French Quarter.

Too bad I wouldn't be able to stay there. Well, probably not anyway, but I hadn't ruled it out completely. I was open to possibilities. I'd try it out for a month or two and see what happened.

I'd found a little furnished room right in the heart of things. It was exactly what I was looking for too: small, convenient, and inexpensive.

When I first walked in and saw the place, I knew it would be perfect, at least for a little while. Nothing fancy, but it had what I needed: a double bed, a couch, and a bathroom. Home. My new home. It even had a third-floor view of Bourbon Street.

I could hear the excitement pouring in through the little window, so I walked over and pushed the curtain aside to check out the view. Throngs of individuals were walking—some staggering—by. I felt like an invisible bird, right in the middle of the place that all those people had come to see.

After I got semi-settled, I rearranged my hair, put some color on my lips, then headed out to explore my surroundings. I had a few job options that I had seen listed in the newspaper; however, as it turned out, I never applied at any of them.

Instead, I stopped in front of a blues club on Bourbon Street named The Blue. The doors were wide open, and the music pouring out captivated and drew me in. Business cards and dollar bills were hanging all along the walls. I instantly felt a connection with the building itself: the brick walls, the concrete floor, the dusty ceiling.

Roger, the manager hired me on the spot. No application or anything. I just started working right away.

He took me over and introduced me to the other two cocktail waitresses: Erica and Jennifer.

Erica had dark hair like mine, and looked like she could have been my sister, or at least a cousin. I felt comfortable with her immediately, as if we had already been friends for a while. We even seemed to talk with the same rhythm.

After showing me which tables I was supposed to wait on, she explained the proper procedure for ordering the drinks and collecting the money. In less than three minutes, I was fully trained.

She told me she had been working there for about a year, and said, "Most of the other employees have worked here at least as long as I have. We're probably the only club on Bourbon Street that can say that."

"Guess I came to the right place then."

She smiled and said, "We've got a pretty good deal here, and as long as we show up and do our work, the managers don't harass us over petty matters, such as drinking on the job."

"You're allowed to drink on the job?"

"It's not officially sanctioned, but the managers look the other way as long as we're not too obvious about it. They have to know though. Whoever's not looking totally pissed off by 2 A.M. is probably drinking . . . or doing something else. Do you drink—or do drugs?" she asked, as if it were an either/or question.

"Drink."

"Good. Me too. Let's get one now before the bartender gets too busy. I'm gonna have a vodka and cranberry."

"That sounds good. I'll have the same."

The club started filling up, and we were pretty busy for the next hour or so. I liked it there. It seemed pretty easy too: bring a drink, get a dollar . . . sometimes more. And people came to relax and enjoy themselves, so that made for a pleasant atmosphere.

Part of my initial warmth and attraction to the place may have also had something to do with Michael, the guitar player. He had smiled at me when I first walked in, and he came over and introduced himself as soon as the band went on break.

I hadn't even dated anybody for about a year. I had been going through a phase where I really just wanted to be friends with everyone, and especially with just moving back to New Orleans, I certainly wasn't planning on immediately hooking up with anyone. But for some reason, when I first saw Michael, something inside me said, "Yes!" without even pausing to think about it.

He told me that he worked at The Blue five nights a week and that he usually picked up gigs somewhere else on the other two nights. I asked how he could go seven nights a week without a night off.

He grinned. "You mean do I party? You see, for me, this *is* the party; this is what I love. I wake up in the afternoon, start practicing; then I come here."

I just stood there, staring at him with a stupid smile on my face, which I wanted to wipe off, but couldn't. Thus far, he was one of the very few people I had ever met who was actually living his dream and loving his job, and I couldn't think of anything to say. But he didn't seem to mind, and he did kiss my hand before going back on stage.

Erica had witnessed the hand kissing and told me, "Watch out for that one."

"What do you mean?"

"You'll see . . . ."

But I didn't see, not then, because I was already floating off into his world. Although it may not have been love at first sight, we did fall into immediate infatuation.

I told him my name was Samantha, but he started calling me *Sammi* from the start. A few times during the night, he even walked up behind me and whispered it—not that he had to. I was constantly aware of him and could feel his presence, even when my back was to him.

It was only my first night there, but I already felt that I belonged. The French Quarter had officially taken me in under her wing.

That night, my first night to sleep in my new room, I had a really vivid dream. I was running down a street, might've been in the French Quarter. It was hard to tell exactly because it was so dark and empty. There weren't even any cars on the street.

I could hear footsteps—someone was chasing me. I felt as if I should probably be scared, but I wasn't. I was laughing.

I woke up abruptly and sat straight up, looking around me, trying to figure out where I was. I felt so strange. I even got up and walked over to the mirror to see what I looked like because, at that moment, I couldn't remember. The dream had felt so real, as if it had actually happened, as if I had really been there. I at least felt as if I'd had that dream before.

A few nights later at work, Michael came up to me at the end of my shift. We just stood there and looked at each other for a moment, smiling, breathing each other in. Then he told me, "Bon soir, mon petit fleur de lis."

I said, "Bon soir," then asked, "You speak French?"

"I listened to some tapes for a while and learned a little bit."

"Your pronunciation is great. You sound fluent."

"Well if you ever go to Paris with me, maybe we can fool them all." He took my hand in his and said, "But for now, let's go to Deja Vu and get something to eat."

I left my hand in his and allowed him to lead me there. Deja vu . . . yeah, that's what he was to me. But in an exciting way, like *Oh, now I remember. This is the boy I adventure with.*

We decided to split a burger and fries. After we ate, I said something, I don't even remember what, but Michael asked, "You're not a local are you?"

I smiled and said, "No. I'm not even from Louisiana, but some of my relatives came from around here, and I always felt that this was probably my true home."

"You've sort of got that Cajun look."

"I do have a little Cajun blood in me."

"What did you do before you came here?"

"I was an English major in college for a few years, but I needed a break, so I took one."

"You got out just in time."

"Why?"

He smiled, raised one eyebrow and said, "You're already starting to look like an English teacher, but I think there's still hope for you."

"Okay . . . whatever that means. Anyway, that's my motto: if you get tired of the locale, change it."

"Absolutely."

"Seriously, I know it sounds cliché, but I mean it. I don't ever want to feel as if I'm stuck somewhere because I have to be. I want to go where I want to and do what I want to do."

He grinned and asked, "Can I go with you?"

I smiled back and said, "I haven't mastered the art of reading the future yet."

He looked at me for a moment as if he were trying to figure me out, then asked, "So where are you from?"

"Right here."

"No, I mean originally."

"Well, I grew up all over, so wherever I am is my home. Just got back from traveling a little bit, but before this, I lived uptown."

"Well, you're far, far away from there. You're not in the United States of America anymore. You're in the French Quarter now."

"What's that supposed to mean?"

"The French Quarter is its own country. There are a lot of people who've grown up here and never left— probably never will leave either unless they're forced out at gunpoint—maybe not even then. There are also people who came here from other places, maybe just to visit even, but then they stayed. There's something about this place."

I smiled and said, "Yes, I've noticed . . . ."

After we finally ran out of things to talk about, he offered to walk me home, and I agreed. He spontaneously picked me up in his arms and carried me several blocks, all the way back to my place.

I invited him in that night, and he ended up crashing on the couch. That was okay. I liked him being there. I liked him.

That became a nightly thing; then I started letting him sleep on the double bed as long as he promised not to make a pass at me. For some reason, the bed had felt small when I had been in it by myself, but now that he was in it with me, it felt plenty big, big enough, just right. Everything felt just right. Platonic still, but that was all right too.

Then one night we got really drunk, came home, and consummated our infatuation.

His roommate situation wasn't working out, so at first I thought that his staying with me was just a temporary thing, even as I saw more of his belongings gradually making their way over to my place. I thought it would be better if we each had our own space and just spent as much time together as we wanted to—even if it was all the time. When I mentioned that to him, he went and looked at one or two places to appease me, then let it slide. I guess I did too.

Besides, we were still enjoying each other. We'd get into these really deep discussions that actually made no sense, but we were just happy to hear our own voices. And he'd play his guitar and sing his originals to me, which I loved. My world fell at his feet when he sang to me.

He and I had one of those rare, instant, connective bonds from the very beginning, or maybe even before the beginning. And when he spoke to me, it almost felt as if I'd already heard whatever it was he had to say—maybe a half second before he said it, or maybe ages ago, who knows? Sort of like an echo, or altered time, combined with a feeling of somehow being more alive.

One night, we stopped in a cozy candlelit bar called Josephine's. I immediately felt at home there.

A couple of guys with a guitar were sitting at the bar, so Michael gravitated toward them.

I ordered drinks and started talking to Josie, the bartender. Turned out she was the owner too. She had long black hair, which she was wearing in two long braids, and was dressed sort of like a medieval princess. I complimented her on her outfit.

She smiled and said, "Thanks, I made it."

"Wow! You made that?"

"Yes. I make all my own clothes, most of them out of velvet and silk."

"That's amazing! Have you ever thought about selling your designs?"

"No," she said, looking embarrassed. "People have asked me before, but honestly I really don't want anyone else wearing my stuff." She smiled and added, "I like to be the only one."

"Well, you are definitely an artist." Her face lit up and she gave me the next drink on the house.

With some people, friendship is a constant effort. With others, it is something that just happens and flows regardless of you or anything that you do. With Josie it was like that from the start. She was offbeat and interesting, but by far, her most endearing trait was that she sincerely seemed to like me.

At some point, one of the guys handed the guitar over to Michael. He embraced it and started playing different songs upon request, including some Janis Joplin and some Hendrix. We sang along to some of it.

After about five or ten minutes, Michael handed them back the guitar, and we started saying our goodbyes. They asked him to do one more song, to play one of his originals.

He sat back down, took the guitar, and played some love song I had never heard before. When he finished, he said that he had just written it for me.

I told him, "I bet you say that to all the girls."

He smiled and said, "Just the ones I like."

2
Uplifted by the Blues

As I walked into work, the band was just starting up. Erica motioned over to the new guitar player on stage and said, "That's not Michael. Is he sick or something?"

I shook my head, gave a half-smile, and said, "He's not playing here anymore."

"You're kidding! Did Roger kick him out?"

"No, but he's probably happy about it. He doesn't much care for Michael."

"So what happened?"

"The other band members said that his solos were too long and that he was always trying to steal the show."

She smiled and said, "Well . . . he does like to solo. Has he found another place to play yet?"

"Yeah, he's moved on to a club down the street where they're not hip to his egomania yet."

"That was quick. Are you gonna try to get a job there too?"

"No. I plan on staying here, for the time being anyway. I like it all right. Not only do I get to hang out and drink for free while listening to great live music, but I'm also getting paid for it and making decent money."

The bands that played there really were very entertaining. One of them had that mean: *We Broke Up Bitch, So What's It To You* blues. The other one had that bee-bop: *My Baby Left Me, So I Found a New Baby* blues. The overall kind of feeling their music gave you was: *Yeah, my baby split and I'm all alone, but if I drink enough and make it rhyme, I can still dance to it.*

There was a little dance floor too, a small area to the right of the stage. Sometimes people would go up there to dance, but a lot of times, someone would just stop there for a minute and dance on their way to the bathroom. We, the employees, never danced up there, although we would sometimes dance in place when we found it impossible not to. No big arm movements or anything like that, just a very subtle, rhythmic thing, of course.

On stage, there was a piano player, a guitarist, a bass player, a drummer, and a horn player—or two or three; it varied. The tables in the club were lined up for community seating in order to pack in as many customers as possible, and they did pack them in there too.

The *We Broke Up Bitch, So What's It To You* band was playing that night. I didn't have many customers yet, so I was checking them out. I liked not only to listen to their music, but also to watch the faces of the musicians as they performed. They all had different expressions they would make while they were playing their instruments.

The bass player, in particular, was very expressive. Doing a solo, he suddenly looked possessed, as if something—or someone—was trying to explode out of his head. Speaking in terms of his face rather than his bodyweight, he had that "I've been fasting in the desert for several months" look, and it appeared as if he had suddenly had a revelation. His music reflected it too.

Katie, one of the bartenders, came over and asked if I wanted a cocktail. I told her, "Sure. The blues and sobriety don't really mix. Even after just one drink, I can always feel the music so much deeper."

She handed me my drink and asked, "Did you ever listen to the blues before you worked here?"

I took a sip and said, "No, and I didn't know if it would depress me, but it doesn't. Now if they played country music here, I would've never come in. That's just not my thing."

"Oh definitely not my thing either."

"But listening to the blues is different. I can feel the blues until—ultimately—it's very uplifting. It takes me to the other side."

Katie fixed herself a drink, took a sip, and said, "I know what you mean. I'm starting to feel uplifted already."

There were two other bartenders working. Seth, the fuzzy guy on the other end, was juggling lemons to amuse his customers. He came across as a pothead, but maybe he was just enlightened.

Dana, the blonde in the middle, was the most imposing. She acted as if she hated everybody—and as if she were happy about it too, but I wasn't sure that was the case.

The customers, waitresses, and bartenders weren't the only ones drinking; the band had their share too. Whereas we would drink our cocktails out of big, sixteen-ounce plastic cups to make it look like we were just drinking water or juice or whatever, the band members would usually drink a shot of Jagermeister, or tequila, or something else small and powerful so that they could finish it quickly between songs.

We all knew how long our shift was, and so we could pace our drinks according to our own personal tolerance levels. In that way, we could stay happy and jolly without getting too messy and obvious. After all, we *were* at work and there was money to be made. I stayed sober enough to work by avoiding drugs and by properly spacing my big drinks of vodka and water, which, to the unsuspecting, just looked like water.

Naturally, there were often some drugs floating around if anyone wanted or needed to partake of any of them. At one point, I told Jennifer, "My little toe hurts. I don't know what I did to it though."

With no hesitation she asked, "Do you want some downers?"

"What kind are they?" I asked, just out of curiosity.

"I don't know; they're green. Someone gave them to me. Do you know what kind are green?"

"No, but I definitely wouldn't take them if you don't know what they are."

She shrugged and said, "I guess you're right. It might get you too messed up to work." She pulled one out of her pocket, looked at it, shrugged again, and popped it into her mouth.

Erica had asked if I wanted to hang out after work, but at the end of the shift, she came over and told me, "I'm not gonna be able to hang out tonight after all."

"What's up?"

"Jennifer. She's so wasted. Usually she doesn't get this bad. I'm trying to cover for her and help her with her closing duties."

"She took some downers."

"Oh, that would explain it. The worst part is that her boyfriend usually drops her off at work, but tonight she drove. So now I have to drive her home.

"Where's she live?"

"The West Bank."

"Ha! Do you need any help with her?"

"Thanks—I've got it covered. Seth's gonna help me."

"Have fun."

Katie was walking by and told me, "Samantha, you can come hang out with us. We're going to Nugent's."

"What's Nugent's?"

Dana walked up and said, "A bar full of locals bitching about the freaks they had to deal with at work that night."

I laughed and headed over with them. At some point, Katie asked me how I had ended up in the French Quarter. Actually, my answer was different every day, depending on who asked the question and what kind of mood I was in. I gave her the short answer about taking some time off school to do some writing.

That was the real answer, but just one version of it. I've discovered that there are many real answers, and that they can change from one day to the next, or even from one minute to the next. That was the answer for *her*.

Michael and I hooked up a little later at his club. After telling him about the night, he asked, "So why did you really move into the Quarter? Why now?"

"Why not now? It seemed as good a time as any. The world has changed—is changing. It seemed kind of silly spending all that time preparing for life within a framework that may not even exist by the time I'm ready for it."

"Yeah, who knows . . . with all these crazy hurricanes and earthquakes, along with the terrorism and war . . . ."

"Yeah, all of that. I'm not saying we should sit around and do nothing because the world's gonna end; I'm saying start doing what we wanna do now, not spend ten years getting ready. The world as we know it may not even exist ten years from now."

"So you really think the world's going to end soon?"

"No, not at all. I just think it's about to change significantly. A lot of the ways we do things don't fit anymore. I think we're about to outgrow them."

"Like what?"

"I don't know exactly. I have more questions than answers."

"Well what kinds of things do you think?"

"Oh, maybe the forty-hour work week. Also, I think the educational system as it exists now was designed for a different place on the time-space continuum."

"I always thought it would be cool if we could learn everything we needed to know while we were sleeping."

"Maybe we do. Or maybe we could—if we knew how. Maybe that's what we should spend time learning in school."

Michael laughed and said, "Hey, I tried, but the teacher always woke me up."

We sat in silence for a moment; then Michael grinned and said, "Yeah, you got out just in time."

"I guess so. You know, I always thought of myself as the kind of person who always did the right thing. Only now I realize—it wasn't necessarily the right thing—just the expected thing, the appropriate thing, the proper thing."

"Looks like that's over now."

"Yeah, at least for the time being. You know, if I'd have stayed in school, I wouldn't be like I am now—lost . . . confused . . . questioning. This is better, really, because if I didn't ask my questions, then I would never find my answers. I'd just accept someone else's answers that might work for them, even if they didn't work for me. I don't want to live anyone else's life. I want to live mine."

"To thine own self be true."

I smiled and said, "Yes. I'll take my twisted path, wherever it may lead me. Even on a really shitty day, I'd still rather be me than anyone else."

3
The Bohemian Palace of Pleasure

The next day, I was thinking about what Michael (and Shakespeare) had said about being true to yourself. Michael certainly was true to himself. He really did do whatever he wanted to. I knew that was why he was with me now, because he wanted to be. Kind of flattering. But I also had the feeling that the moment he wanted to be with some other girl that he would be too. But anyway, it's not like I had any intention of getting married or anything anytime soon, so I decided not to worry my pretty little head over it. I'd deal with that when and if it came up.

He came and met me after work that night. I made him wait outside so his presence wouldn't antagonize Roger. Granted it didn't take much to antagonize Roger, but he was always very nice to me.

On the way over to Deja Vu, Michael asked me, "Do you know what today is?"

"Wednesday—no wait! It's after midnight, so it's Thursday."

"True. But it's Thanksgiving too."

"Oh yeah, that. And I forgot to bake a turkey."

"That's okay. In the French Quarter, we celebrate the holiday appropriately with shots of Wild Turkey, followed by cranberry chasers."

After a couple of those, I asked Michael, "So, what are you thankful for this Thanksgiving?"

"Wild Turkey and twenty-four hour bars!"

I laughed, and we toasted that; then I said, "I'm grateful that I didn't have to sit through Thanksgiving this year . . . that I didn't go home for the whole ordeal. From now on, I think I'll just call New Orleans my home. I feel so much freer here, so much more me."

"I feel free too. I feel like I have wings, but I can't fly, you know? I'm floating only in the mind, not in the body."

On that note, we had another shot, then floated on home.

We had moved into a large studio-style attic apartment. It was in the Quarter, but it was over in the gay residential area, removed from the tourist tract. We were able to get a much bigger space over there for the same price that we had been paying for that tiny noisy room in the middle of the chaos.

It was good. I was ready for a place where I could come stretch out, and breathe, and maybe even hear myself think. And it was still close enough to everywhere we needed or wanted to go.

As we lay down, I told Michael, "The first morning light. Ha. That's usually the last thing I see before I go to sleep."

"Yeah, while half the world is waking up, we're just drifting off."

We had the window open, and I could smell croissants from the bakery down the street. It's funny how a certain smell or scent can take you back to a memory. Burgundy wine does that. Sometimes I even like the smell of dirty hair on a stranger. For me, that croissant smell will always remind me of the time I lived in the French Quarter.

When I woke up that afternoon, Michael was already awake. He knelt beside me, caressed my face, and told me, "Stay here. I'll be right back."

He headed down to the deli on the corner to get our coffee, which he did just about every day. Of course it would have been much more practical to buy a coffeepot and make our own, but we were hardly practical, and besides, that was a little more domestically inclined than we wanted to be.

While I waited for him, I just rested and looked around. I really did love our new place. The kitchen had a skylight, and both the kitchen and the bathroom had black and white tile floors. In between was a big room with beige carpet and a high ceiling.

From that large, multi-purpose room where we lived and slept, big French windows opened out onto a sloping roof, and the roof connected to the adjacent buildings. They were all like that really: I think all the buildings on our block had one big connecting rooftop. From there, we could see hundreds of French Quarter rooftops, with the Central Business District in the background and the Mississippi Bridge off to the left.

Our furnishings that we had managed to acquire consisted of a double mattress on the floor, a rattan couch, a coffee table we had painted indigo blue, a small black-and-white TV painted a multitude of colors, and a pedestal fan—also multi-colored.

Books were randomly piled in messy stacks along the walls. They seemed to have a life of their own and migrated around different parts of the room according to mood. I'd occasionally attempt to put them all in one spot in some type of organized manner, but inevitably they'd just stretch and shuffle and spread out again. I finally gave up. My books went where they wanted to.

After Michael got back, we decided to go do laundry since we had nothing decent left to wear. We always wore some outdated or ridiculous clothes to the laundromat because all of our good clothes were dirty by then. I put on some out-of-style pants and a pink tee shirt that said, "I'm Chrissy. Fly me." I thought it was especially funny since my name wasn't Chrissy. I had found it in some second-hand store.

Michael, looking rather retro himself, hoisted the giant laundry bag over his shoulder, and we started heading over to the laundromat on the next block.

I told him, "It's times like this that it's nice to have a man around."

He grinned, raised the eyebrow and said, "You could make it even nicer if you went to get us a couple of beers."

Obligingly, I stopped at the deli and got two sixteen-ounce bottles, then headed over to meet Michael. He had already started the wash and was talking to Tony, the laundry clerk.

Tony was more feminine than I am, or anybody else I know for that matter. He was always flitting around, dancing, twirling, singing, "I am so beautiful," as well as tunes from various Broadway and off-Broadway productions. When I walked in, he spun around in a pirouette and said, "Sister Woman! With the Budweiser! I'll trade you this purple kite in exchange for a beer."

Michael said, "Cool! We can hang it up over our bed."

I laughed and said, "Bed, mattress, whatever," picturing our mattress on the floor. I really didn't care about the kite, but Tony was even more entertaining with a beer in him, so I was happy to provide. He was worth it. I went back across the street to the deli and got another beer so we could all have one, our first anyway. We always drank when we did laundry, and Tony provided the entertainment.

When we got back home, we spent more time hanging up the kite than we did on the laundry; we just poured the clothes out on the mattress and spread them around a little bit. Then Michael got ready and left for work.

I still had a little time before I had to go in, so I went and sat out on the roof. I could see a barge floating by, and at my location, three stories up, it seemed to be almost eye-level. I knew it had something to do with the New Orleans sea-level. Still, it seemed bizarre, as if my eyes were deceiving me somehow, sort of like an Escher print.

A horse and buggy turned on our street and went right past our building, transporting tourists. I held my hand up to block out the downtown buildings in the background, and for a moment, I imagined that I was back in nineteenth-century New Orleans.

Twenty-first century sounds quickly hurtled me back into the present. A block away, I could see and hear two guys threatening to fight: one in his car almost hit the other on foot. The one on foot yelled menacingly, "You wanna get out of the car and say that to my face, muthafucker?" Apparently the driver didn't, because he sped off.

The little old lady in the renovated pink and gray house across the street came out to find her cats. Her fenced in yard was beautiful and immaculately kept. I watched her for a little while and tried to imagine what it would be like to be her: to live an apparently normal life in a normal house in the middle of the not-so-normal French Quarter. I tried to picture myself living in her house as an old woman, walking out into that big, beautiful yard looking for my cats.

Some guy walking down the street below was singing, "In Dixie Land I'll take my stand to live and die in Dixie." Every time he'd sing, "Look away," he'd turn his head in an exaggerated manner. He was just walking by himself, singing as loudly as he could.

I suddenly wondered if I would get old and die there, or if I would just die there, not even wait to get old. I involuntarily shivered. Then I thought: *That's ridiculous. I'll die when and where I want to, and I'll live as long as I want to until then.*

It was starting to get dark, so I went in to shower and get ready for my night, the way most people get ready for their day.

When I got to work a little while later, I told Erica about my new place.

She said, "You pass right by my apartment on your way to work. I'm on Bourbon Street, just a couple of blocks from you. Are you working tomorrow?"

"Yes."

"You should stop by my place. We can walk to work together."

I agreed, so she wrote her address on a coaster and handed it to me, saying, "Come by early, and you can stop in for a drink."

The next night, I went to her building and looked inside the gate at the courtyard. That was actually one of my new hobbies: peeking in at courtyards in the Quarter. I never knew what elegant well-maintained vistas or run-down decrepit beauty I might see. Her courtyard really was pretty, with a gorgeous fountain and lush greenery.

I rang the bell so she could buzz me in, then went upstairs to her apartment. The first thing I noticed and loved in it was the black and white tile floor. The second thing was the dark wood furniture.

"Erica, your place is gorgeous!"

"Come on in and I'll show you the rest of it."

Her bedroom had a black iron canopy bed with white sheer fabric draped across the top of it. I ran my fingers along one of the posts and told her, "I've always dreamed about having a bed like this."

She smiled. "That was probably the biggest purchase I ever made in my life, but I had to have it. Now I don't know if I like this one better, or the other one. Come see."

The second bedroom had a four-poster mahogany bed with a white Matelassé cover on top.

I gasped. "I see what you mean."

She pulled some drapes aside and said, "Come check out the view from the balcony."

There was a white wicker couch out there and a white wrought iron table with two chairs. There were also several hanging fern plants. That's one thing I had first noticed upon my arrival in New Orleans: If you live in Louisiana, you really should have at least one hanging fern.

She motioned for me to step out there and said, "We still have plenty of time. Have a seat and I'll get you a drink."

I sat on the wicker couch. The view was great. It was at the part of Bourbon Street where it was still a little touristy, but it was starting to calm down. It was at that dividing line between residential and tourist.

Erica came back out with a vodka and water for me and a vodka and cranberry for her. She sat next to me on the couch and put her feet up on the little coffee table in front of it.

I told her, "This place is incredible! Do you have another job I don't know about, or do you just make a lot more money than I do at work?"

"Neither. Actually, I used to have a roommate, and when she left, she sold me most of this furniture—cheap too, because she didn't want to take it with her. I tried to find another roommate and couldn't . . . well, not one I liked anyway. So I thought I was going to have to move, but then someone hooked me up with another plan."

"Sugar Daddy?"

She laughed. "No. Instead of having a roommate year-round, a couple of times a year—for big events, such as Mardi Gras and Jazz Fest and stuff like that, I stay at a friend's place, lock up my bedroom, and rent the rest of my apartment out. The money I make off that helps me pay the rent the rest of the year."

"Well you have the perfect place for it. This balcony's wonderful, and that's great that you can keep your bedroom separate."

"Yeah, anything that I don't want anybody messing with, I just push in there and lock it up before I go. So far, it's been working out great."

"You're welcome to stay at my place for Mardi Gras if you want."

"Thanks, but I already made plans to stay at Katie and Danny's."

"Who's Danny?"

"The bass player. He and Katie live together."

"Oh, I didn't realize that."

"That's because they were separated for a little while, but they just got back together."

"Well I hope he treats her well. Katie's so sweet."

"Yeah, she almost seems too innocent for the French Quarter scene."

"Yeah, but in another way, it seems as if it's all she's ever known. Like to her, the French Quarter scene is both normal and innocent."

She finished her drink and said, "You know, I never thought of it like that, but it's true. Anyway, we'd better get going."

We stuck our glasses in the sink in the kitchen and went downstairs. As we headed to work, I asked her, "So, what's Dana's story?"

"Oh, your typical bad parents, runaway child scenario. She was the oldest, so I think she actually stuck it out there until she was around sixteen or so; then she'd still sneak back home every once in a while to help her younger brothers."

"If you need a big sister to protect you, she'd be a good one."

"No kidding."

"Well maybe not for me though. She doesn't seem to like me all that much."

"That's because she doesn't like Michael. She judges you by your company."

"What kind of fair is that?"

"Well I don't dislike Michael. I just don't trust him. I don't judge you for that, though. Hey, are you working tomorrow?"

"No, I'm off. How about you?"

"Working. Any exciting plans?"

"No. I'll probably hang out with Michael until he goes to work. Maybe go to A&P at some point."

"And get what? What do you eat?"

"Oh, I don't know. I just grab the simplest looking things and get out."

"That's what I do too. If I see a jar of salsa next to the chips, I'll grab it—rather than go to the actual salsa aisle and have to choose from the ever-increasing assortment."

"Exactly. I'm the same way with clothes. I walk in a store and just get it over with as quickly as possible."

"Me too. I think it's the lighting in retail stores. If they made a clothing store that looked more like a dimly-lit bar, I'd probably feel more comfortable there."

"And maybe grocery shop by candlelight?"

"In the middle of the night."

"Now you're talking."

When we walked into work, Roger said, "Here's Double-Trouble! Are y'all carpooling now?"

We laughed and told him that we had walked in together, that we were on the same route. It did seem fitting too. Customers were always asking if we were sisters, and sometimes they'd even think we were twins. It did seem more like we were siblings than friends.

And so, I blended into residential life in the Quarter and became a local. Or at least I covered the same ground and did some of the same things that other locals did—those who lived and worked in the Quarter and didn't have a car.

There were certain parts of certain streets that I walked on every day. It almost seemed as if my footsteps should've worn a path in the pavement. Still, there were other parts of the Quarter that my shoe soles never touched. I pretty much stayed between Bourbon and Decatur, and I spent as little time as possible in the first couple blocks of Bourbon off Canal.

Ironically, those first couple blocks were the first impression that the Canal-hotel-staying-tourists got of the French Quarter, and it couldn't have been a very good one. It set the stage for what they were expecting as they wandered deeper in.

In reality, the deeper and further down Bourbon Street one wanders, the tamer and more normal it becomes. Sometimes, if I woke up early enough, I'd even see the school bus dropping kids off after school.

Sure, there were aspects of the Quarter that were criminal and sometimes violent. Understandably, that's what some people didn't like about it.

However, other aspects exuded a quiet, delicate beauty, an indescribable something, a *j'en sais quois* that somehow seemed like home to me. Maybe I'd see it in some architecture or in some art or in a piece of mahogany . . . or even in someone's eyes when I could see that they loved it there just as much as I did and probably for the same reasons.

Oh God. I had already fallen in deep, and it was just the beginning . . . .

4

Christmas in the Quarter

As Christmas approached, there were hardly any tourists in the French Quarter. The majority of the shops, restaurants, and music bars had shut down. Some closed for a few days; some closed for the entire month. Strains of music from the few remaining clubs could be heard all the way down the block, or further, amidst the encompassing silence.

Usually the multitude of sounds bounced off one another; now the few existing sounds were just slowly drifting out of range. Although the suburban malls were filled with high-spirited crowds of Christmas shoppers, the tourist magnets in the Quarter were practically vacant, occupied solely by the bored cashiers and sales people.

To me, the French Quarter actually seemed more like a residential community around Christmas than it normally did. Heading over to my favorite used bookstore one evening, I came upon thousands of people gathered together in Jackson Square for a candlelight caroling service. As I paused to check it out, someone handed me a white candle and a song sheet, and I soon found myself singing along songs that I knew by heart, with tears forming in my eyes. It reminded me of the better parts of my childhood. I was no longer religious, but I was sentimental, and I did like to sing.

I decided not to go the bookstore afterward. Instead, I went and got some hot chocolate at Café du Monde and strolled through the French Quarter, looking at all the decorations. I loved the pretty little lights outlining the wrought-iron balconies.

Walking home, I saw two male homeless men sleeping wrapped in each other's arms—one with his head stuck in the other guy's jacket. It looked as if they were just huddled together for warmth.

I know some people probably don't think that it gets very cold in New Orleans, especially if they've ever visited there in the summer, but that humidity can go either way. It can make summer hotter and winter colder—creating a damp, bone-chilling cold that can make it hard to warm up. I was grateful I had a warm place to go home to.

The next day, I talked Michael into bundling up and going over to the French Market with me to pick out a Christmas tree. We bought the biggest one we could find and carried it home in our arms, singing "Jingle Bells" and "We Wish You a Merry Christmas" the whole way. We got smiles and waves, and a few people even sang a few notes along with us.

We managed to get the tree upstairs to our apartment; then we decorated it with beverage coasters, business cards, and earrings. To further enhance the décor, I draped a feather boa someone had given us across the rattan couch.

Michael sat down on the indigo coffee table and started playing his guitar. While he expanded his chord-vocabulary vowels, I stretched out on the floor to relax my body through meditation and open my mind for thought. When we were sufficiently expanded and relaxed, we decided to go for a walk.

We stopped at Central Grocery on Decatur and got half a Muffaletta sandwich to-go and a bottle of red wine, then went and had a little evening picnic at the river.

For some reason, I felt a little off. After we had taken our last bite and poured another glass of wine, I attempted to describe the premenstrual angst I was experiencing to Michael. "I feel as if I'm the only one who can solve all the world's problems, and I was supposed to do it yesterday. Or, as if I have finals tomorrow and I haven't been to class all semester. I feel like I have to know everything, and I have to know it right now: where I'm going next, where I'm going after that, and what I'm going to do when I get there."

Without even flinching, Michael said, "That's not PMS, baby, that's the alignment of the planets. I feel it too."

I smiled and said, "I've never met anyone like you before."

With a serious look, he grasped my hand and said, "I've never met anyone like you either. I didn't know anyone like you even existed."

"Good," I said, "Because I don't want to be like anyone else."

"See, that's the thing, Sammi, most people *do* want to be like everyone else because they want to fit in."

"I don't need to fit in, like some others do." Then I smiled and added, "Although it's okay when it works out the way, when the birds of *my* feather have flocked together."

"You are a poet. Can I be your muse?"

"Well, you already do inspire me in some ways. So, sure, you can be my muse, for the time being anyway."

He impulsively kneeled in front of me and said, dreamily, "Let's get married and I'll be your muse forever."

I pulled him up, looked deep into his eyes, and said, "I'm not that conventional, but my heart will be with you every day that I am."

A few nights later, I called Bianca, my former college roommate, to catch up on her news and to share some of mine. After the requisite Merry Christmas/Happy New Year salutation, I told her about our new apartment: "The whole feeling of the place is light, spacious, and airy. I immediately named it *The Bohemian Palace of Pleasure*."

She laughed and said, "You always name your places. First, there was *Galahad's Pad*, then *The Sleaze Motel*, now *The Bohemian Palace*."

"Actually I think you named *Galahad's Pad*. And it was appropriate too, what with everybody always crashing over there, more people coming than going."

"Yeah, we'd wake up in the morning and see people we didn't even know sleeping on the floor. It's not like that where I am now. I hardly even see my current roommate; we just leave each other notes. I've gone from *Galahad's Pad* to *The Notepad*."

"And I've moved on to *The Bohemian Palace of Pleasure*."

"Nothing wrong with pleasure. Are you having fun?"

"Yes, but I think Michael's getting serious."

"Well, whatever you do, don't go falling in love with him; you'll never make it back to school. Is it too late? Do you already love him?"

"Maybe. What does love mean anyway?"

"You're kidding, right?"

"No, not really. I mean, do I like him? Yes, most of the time. Do I feel passionate about him in a physical way? Definitely. Does he inspire me as an individual? Yes, in certain ways. Do I want to spend the rest of my life with him? I don't know."

"Well I wouldn't rush into marriage then."

"Marriage? Yeah, right. I don't think that's really my thing. But I can't imagine my life without him right now. I feel like we're together for some project or purpose or inspiration or something. Then again, maybe we're just killing time."

"I know what you mean. Sometimes I think 'I love you' just means 'I like you better than any of my other choices right now.' "

I laughed and said, "Sometimes it doesn't even mean 'I like you.' Anyway, I'll try to shake him loose by August. In the meantime, I've got to enjoy my life."

"So are you still planning on making it back to school next fall?"

"Maybe. Yeah probably. I don't know. All I know is that I have to be here right now. There's some compelling reason; I'm just not sure what it is yet. Anyway, I have a few more minutes to talk, then I have to go to work."

"Are you still working at the same place?"

"Yeah, why not? It's better than any of the other choices around here, and I really like it most of the time."

"Have you replaced me yet with a tell-all confidante female friend?"

"Darling, you are irreplaceable; however, I have made a few friends here."

"Well good. I'm not jealous, as long as you keep me in the loop."

"Are you kidding? You are the loop; you invented the loop; you crocheted the loop!"

"Well be sure and let me know if you get married or pregnant or anything."

"Yeah, right."

"It could happen."

"It won't happen."

I hung up the phone, got dressed, and left—still thinking about what she had said. Pregnant? No.

Well, my period was late, but I hadn't told her that. No reason to jump to conclusions; I was often irregular.

5

Forget Que Sera

It was almost midnight and I was getting ready to go out. It was earlier than usual anyway. The sole of one of my boots had come apart at the big toe, and it flapped a little when I walked. I sat down and super-glued it, then stood up and tried to walk only to discover that I was unable to lift my big toe. Damn! I had accidentally super-glued my sock to my boot. I quickly remedied the situation, then headed out.

In fact, I was not pregnant, and I figured that was worth celebrating. Granted, I usually didn't need any excuse to celebrate.

I arrived at Michael's *club du jour* to watch his band play some tunes. All the clubs on Bourbon Street had house bands, but Michael seemed to be playing with a different one just about every week. He wasn't much of a team player.

I could kind of understand it though. Some people weren't meant to be followers, couldn't be followers, had to do their own thing—even if it meant doing it alone. Yes, I could understand it because he and I may have been dancing together, but we were each dancing to the beat of our own drummer.

The club gave last call, so I decided to leave while they counted out their money and got paid. It was just as well because the manager was in one of his violently angry moods. Some indignant customer had refused to sign his credit card voucher after running up a five-hundred dollar bar tab. They'd called the cops, but in the meantime, it wasn't a pretty scene. I decided not to stick around.

I walked over to a little bar around the corner to wait. I never liked to go in there when it was crowded, but semi-empty it was pretty cool. Only six other people were in there, as well as a couple of fruit flies that kept circling my bourbon and 7-up.

For some reason, I felt strange. I was only on my first drink, but ever since I'd had a lucid dream that afternoon, possibly an out-of-body experience, I felt like I was in an altered state. I'm not sure what it was exactly, not paranoia, perhaps just an enhanced perception or awareness: like I'd see something out of the corner of my eye and jump, only to discover immediately that it was just one of my eyelashes.

We were listening to Tchaikovsky on the jukebox. I really like Tchaikovsky; however, it's the last thing I would have expected to hear in a bar like that. I looked around at the other six people and wondered which one of them might have played it. Appearances aren't everything, I know, but I couldn't picture any of them choosing classical music. Maybe someone had put it on by mistake.

I suddenly smelled a different odor. Either the person next to me had gas, or the stuff in the sewage was backing up. If it was the sewage, he probably thought I had gas. I really needed some fresh air! I took a walk outside and went over to the corner by the Lucky Dog man to see if Michael was approaching. He wasn't.

A couple of guys slowed down and eyed me up and down. Either they thought I was attractive, or they were wondering why I thought it would be okay to wear my old super-glued go-go boots with some vintage dress. Anyway, I ignored them. I dressed according to mood and whim, and didn't feel compelled to follow the weekly or monthly dictates of fashion.

I went back in the bar and sat on a stool. A few more people had come in. A guy offered to buy me a drink, but I told him I didn't need one, and it was actually true. I was starting to feel a little lightheaded. It was only my second drink, but in addition to feeling strange anyway, I wasn't used to bourbon.

Vodka had been my drink for a while, but I was tired of it and searching for a reasonable substitute. Bourbon was definitely not it . . . . Oh well, maybe there was no substitute for vodka. The taste was so smooth and the smell practically imperceptible, unlike bourbon, which was rough and throaty, with a smell that jumped out at you and almost knocked you over.

I felt someone intently staring at me outside the window, so I turned to look. Some man I didn't even know winked at me and continued staring. *Go away, freaky man!*

Michael finally came, and we went to Josephine's. Josie fixed our drinks right away, but the bar was crowded, so she moved on down the line.

She had her dark hair in braids, as usual, but they were pinned up on the top of her head. It sort of gave her a French maiden look. And maiden was a good word for her too, because although she was strong and self-confident, she had an elegant femininity about her. She could handle the bar by herself, and throw someone out if she needed to, but she wouldn't say a single curse word while she was doing it.

A friend of Michael's came over and started talking to us. He was already very drunk, but he bought us a drink, then started talking about his wife and asked us to call her up and tell her he loved her.

Michael gave him a serious look, clasped his hand, and said, "You do it man. You call her up and tell her you love her!"

The man looked horrified and said, "I'm a real man. I carry power tools! I can't tell a woman I love her. You call her up please! Call her up and tell her I love her."

Apparently, they had separated again. He slurred to us that he had been offered an offshore job in Africa and that he'd always wanted to go there, but it would be for a year and that's what his wife was all pissed off about.

He left, and we tried to figure out the words to "I Got You, Babe." Josie was walking by and told us, "There's a version of it by the Pretenders in the Jukebox."

A woman sitting next to me at the bar handed me a dollar to play some music, so I asked her what she wanted to hear.

"Play 'Gypsies, Tramps and Thieves.' Cher does it."

When it came on, she turned to me and said, "In my time, I've been a gypsy, a tramp, and a thief."

I laughed and said, "All three?"

"Yeah. I'm not any of those things anymore, but I guess they're all still a part of me."

"Part of your tapestry."

"Yeah. I guess everything I've been through has influenced who I am today."

"It sounds as if you've had an interesting life."

"I have."

"Well I don't know that I have yet, but I intend to."

She looked at me as if noticing me for the first time and said, "You're young. You have time."

It felt like the beginning of an interesting conversation. Right about then, I looked over and noticed that Michael was almost passed out drunk at the bar. Oh well . . . . I rolled my eyes to Josie and asked her to call us a cab.

The driver that came had driven us before. He was a philosophy major at University of New Orleans, and I always enjoyed talking to him. Michael managed to walk to the cab, but as soon as he got in, he slumped down in the seat and closed his eyes.

Sly and the Family Stone's version of "Que Sera" was playing on the radio.

I looked around me, laughed, and told the driver, "I guess this is my 'Que Sera.'"

He said, "Maybe so," then added, "The future may not be ours to see, but maybe we are creating it right now, each thing we do leading to the next."

"Well that would mean we could still change it, right?"

He laughed. "I hope so."

As he turned onto our street, I asked, "What about the past? Can we change that?"

He stopped in front of my building and said, "You know, I've thought about that before. But if we could go back into the past to change the present, would we even know the difference? Ever know that there had been a road taken, then not taken? Or would we just remember one road, and not remember that there had ever been another?"

"Interesting question," I said, as I paid him and tried to wake Michael up. "Hey, I wonder if I already went back and changed it, and this is what I chose to change it to, for whatever reason. What if I changed it up to this point—and just stepped into this moment now?"

"Well, then this moment here is your starting point. I've heard that all time is simultaneous, that the experience of linear time is an illusion: beginning, middle, end. Whichever moment your consciousness is in right now is your starting point."

After another unsuccessful attempt to wake Michael, I asked the driver, "Could you please help me?"

We managed to get Michael half-awake; then the driver walked in with us to make sure we made it all the way up the stairs. I tried to pay him extra at that point. He told me, "Nah. Keep your money. It's not everybody I can have a conversation like this with . . . . But forget Que Sera. You create your own future."

6

Follow Your Daydreams

The next night, as I reached Erica's place on my way to work, she burst out the door and said, "Guess what? I've got news!"

"What's up?"

She fell into stride beside me and said, "I went out with Jake," referring to the drummer at our club.

"Really? I didn't even know you were interested in him."

"Well, I didn't know he was interested in me either." She grinned and added, "But he is!"

"So tell me all about it!"

"Well I'm trying to take it slow. We were both off work last night, and he took me out to dinner."

"Where did y'all go?"

"Napoleon House."

"That's a romantic place."

"We didn't even kiss!" she said, as if she were confessing something. Then she smiled and added, "But I really get the feeling that he likes me . . . and I like him too."

"Well, taking it slow is a good idea. I definitely wouldn't recommend living together right away."

She laughed and said, "I wouldn't even consider it."

"I never thought I would, but it happened. Michael and I never officially agreed to move in together. It was sort of an extended temporary arrangement that has stagnated into seeming togetherness."

"Do you mind if I learn from your mistakes?"

"Just as long as one of us does."

We walked in silence for a little bit, then she asked me, "So seriously, do you think I'm making a mistake going out with a musician?"

"Definitely. Absolutely!" She laughed, and I continued on, saying, "But at least Jake appears stable, and he's got his steady gig."

She smiled. "That's because he's boring."

"He's not boring."

"Well, he's not a superstar like Michael is." She laughed and added "in his mind."

"Hey, his outer world will catch up with his inner world one of these days. I respect his ambition . . . . But it's probably easier to be with people who are satisfied with where they are."

She shrugged and said, "Yeah . . . but maybe a little boring?"

"That's okay, darling. You crush on your boring boy. I can see you're into him."

When we walked into work, there were hardly any people there yet. Typical Wednesday. Erica was the only one who had any customers.

After setting up my station, I strolled over to the open door and planted myself against the doorframe to see if there was anything interesting walking by on Bourbon Street.

Katie came over and joined me. We just stood there in silence for a moment looking out; then she observed, "You can recognize the foreign tourists right away because they all have skinny legs but pooch tummies since they wear their money belts in front, underneath their shirts."

I added, "Maybe American businessmen should try that. They all have fat butts because they carry their wallets—loaded with $100 bills—in their back pockets. They might as well tape a sign on their back that says, 'Please Rob Me.'"

Dana came over just as two pooch-bellied European tourists walked up to us. Their hair was as blonde as Dana's. They were nervously checking her out. One of them said, "We are from Sweden. We are looking for fun and want girls."

Naively, Katie smiled and told them, "Oh, then go to The Cat's Meow. It's a lot of fun—they have karaoke. It's just a few blocks up."

Looking embarrassed but determined, the guy persisted earnestly, saying, "We want more . . . than that."

Dana, having her own little fun, told them, "Oh, then go to Georgia's," and proceeded to give them directions, sending them to a transvestite bar with very beautiful look-alikes.

The guy asked, "Will we get robbed there?"

She told him, "Just make sure you keep your hand in your pocket and on your wallet because someone could feel you up and take your money, and you'd never even know it until later."

Looking as genuinely naive as possible, the guy asked, "Really?"

She looked at him like he was stupid and said, "Are you kidding? That's the oldest trick in the book! That one goes back to the beginning of time."

After they walked off, Dana laughed and said, "The guys at Georgia's look so much like girls that they'll probably never even know the difference."

A few minutes later, a guy walked up to us and specifically asked me, "Do you know where The Dungeon is? I figured if anyone here would know, it would be you."

Maybe he said it because of my black eyeliner. I only wore it on the top lid, and that night I had extended it out a little further than usual. And my clothes were black. Anyway, although The Dungeon wasn't really my scene, he was right; I did know where it was. I gave them directions, and they went on their way.

By then, the band was getting ready to start back up, so we went back to our stations. The bee-bop: *My Baby Left Me, So I Found a New Baby* band was playing. The lead singer was a petite blonde, but when she sang, she sounded much larger and much more soulful than she actually appeared. Customers were always surprised at the way she looked when they came inside, after hearing her voice booming out to the street.

In drunken incoherence, a tourist woman was screaming and slurring, "Play that one: 'I bought you seven children and now you wanna give them back'! Play that one and I'll give you ten bucks! I'm lyin'—five. Please play it! I'm a tourist. Give me a break."

They didn't know that one, so they did a Saffire The Uppity Blues Women song: "I need a young, young man to chase away my middle age blues."

At that point, the tourist woman literally grabbed a little man sitting behind her, practically abducting him— had he not been so surprised and pleased—and pulled him up on the dance floor. It didn't take us long to recognize that she was dancing in fierce imitation of somebody; we just weren't sure who it was. We finally decided she must be the female Jim Morrison.

Later, another drunken woman fell down on the dance floor as she was heading to the bathroom. Over the microphone Jake said, "Another one bites the dust." In a deeper, lower voice he added, "And don't think nobody noticed."

I had never heard him talk on the microphone before, but he was sort of buzzing from his new romance with Erica, and I think he mainly just said it to try to get her attention. It worked. She looked up at him and smiled. He smiled back at her and winked.

At some point, a schoolteacher-looking couple came in and sat at the bar. Roger sat down next to them and actually had a drink with them. I couldn't believe it. I had never once seen him drink before, and for some reason, I just thought he didn't.

I asked Erica about it. She said, "Yeah, he usually doesn't because he takes painkillers all the time. He must be out of them."

"What does he take them for, just for fun?" I asked, smiling, because it really didn't seem as if he did anything just for fun.

"He says he takes them for some old injury he got when he was in the military."

"Are those his friends?" I asked, nodding toward the couple at the bar.

She laughed and said, "Customers. They come every couple of months to let it all loose in the City of Sin."

"This must be their night."

"Must be."

I guess Roger liked them because they were white (that seemed to be important to him), they spent a lot of money, and they dressed appropriately (although a little while later, they didn't act it). They drank round after round of wine spritzers. Then they decided it was time to leave; however, they didn't leave soon enough. While they were waiting for a cab, the wife started dancing very erotically, like a novice stripper, all the while still wearing her hair in that damn schoolteacher bun.

As they headed out, Jennifer came over and said, "Yeah, she's taking him back to the hotel room to wear him out."

I looked over as the woman stumbled out the door and said, "More like pass out."

Guess they didn't act like that back home. Oh well, that's the reason a lot of people liked to come to New Orleans. They could act entirely different than they normally did. We saw it so often that it almost seemed boring.

After work, a few of us headed over to Nugent's. Katie and Dana were playing video games, Erica was sitting at the bar very close to Jake, and Seth and I were standing off to the side talking. He asked me, "So how do you like working at The Blue so far?"

I hesitated, then told him, "The music is awesome, and the drinking-free part is cool, but sometimes I feel like I got into a Time Machine and went back in time."

"What makes you say that?"

"Well, for one thing, the way our management won't hire anyone black. Roger actually had the audacity to say, 'I've had one opinion about *those* people all my life, and I'm not going to change now.' He didn't even act embarrassed to say it; rather, it seemed as if he were bragging."

"I don't know how he gets away with that. I guess if anyone actually took him to court over it, he wouldn't say anything like that there."

"Probably not. Although if the judge felt the same way as Roger did, he could say whatever he wanted, and it wouldn't matter."

"Unfortunately, that is true."

"Also, the other night, you weren't there, but they had a guest band, and the lead singer interrupted his show every once in a while to put women down and make little demeaning jokes. He went on about how women should just look pretty, and serve him, and not try to talk about anything intelligent."

"Yeah, I've seen him before and caught his spiel. He's definitely not a feminist. Are you?"

"Oh gosh, I don't know. I never really thought about it or looked into it. I generally try to steer clear of any labels. I feel they limit me."

"Labels can be limiting."

"Yeah, I'm always changing. I don't want to be restricted by something I thought I was yesterday. Besides, a particular label can mean different things to different people. Essentially, I feel that all people are equal, regardless of gender or race. I feel that way so completely that I don't understand how anyone could feel differently, although apparently a lot of people do."

"Well, I generally try to be gentle with people and give them the benefit of the doubt. Some really don't know any better. But whenever anybody shows any indication that they *would* like to know better, I'm happy to help guide them in another direction."

I smiled and said, "Great! You can be my guru."

"You don't need a guru. Be your own guru."

"See, that's the kind of statement that shows how wise you truly are, Seth. But you're right. I'm not looking for a guru. I'm just trying to find my own path."

"Trying to find your own path is what puts you on the path. It's the people who don't care that never find it, well not in this life anyway. We all find it sooner or later. The important thing is to stay in your power and try to help lift others up. Don't let the lower energies pull you down."

"It helps talking to you, Seth. I don't think there's anyone else here that I could have had this conversation with."

"Anytime. Hey, I have a CD in my car that I could lend you if you'd like to listen to it."

"Sure, that'd be great. I'm just about ready to leave anyway."

"I'll give you a ride home, and you can take it with you."

When we got in his car, he asked, "Do you ever meditate?"

"I do sometimes. At least I think I do. I lie down on the floor, close my eyes, and try to concentrate on nothing except for my breathing. A lot of times, though, my mind starts wandering."

"That's completely normal." He parked in front of my building and handed me the CD. "This might help though. It's called a guided meditation. It's not actually true meditation, but it will help you with your concentration, which could then improve your meditation."

"Cool. What do I do?"

"Just lay down, same as you do when you're meditating, close your eyes, and listen, trying to concentrate on nothing else but the words on the CD. If you notice that your mind has started wandering, just gently guide it back. It gets easier with practice."

After I thanked him, we just looked at each other for a comfortable moment; then I went inside. The most remarkable thing about Seth was his eye contact. When he looked at me, I felt as if he really saw me, and I could really see him too. He was fully present in his body and seemed fully alive.

When I woke up the next day, he was on my mind. I wasn't attracted to him physically, and he wasn't my type at all, yet I felt an attraction toward him as a person, a human being.

He was the first metaphysical person I'd met. Guess he wasn't a pothead after all. He was really enlightened, or at least on his way.

I put in the guided meditation CD that he had given me, stretched out on the floor, and closed my eyes. It was all about peace and finding peace, and it took me along on some journey up a beautiful path by a river.

Just as I finished listening to it, the phone rang. It was Bianca. I told her that I had just finished meditating.

"Like my ex taught us to?"

"No. I do that sometimes too, but this is a guided meditation CD that some guy at work gave me."

"Any interest there?"

"Just as a friend."

We talked a little more; then I told her that I was about to head over to Jackson Square.

"Oh cool. Do you go there often?"

"Yeah, pretty often. It's one of my favorite places to hang out and people-watch."

"It's just a big open square, right?"

"No, that's one of the things I like about it. It's compartmentalized. There's an inner and outer part, with people hidden, tucked, or propped throughout, however best suits their purpose. Of course anyone trying to make money is positioned conspicuously along the outside of the fence."

"Making money doing what?"

"The horse and buggy carriages are lined up along Decatur, the artists are usually along St. Ann, the tarot card readers are lined up at little tables on Chartres in front of the cathedral, and musicians are sprinkled throughout."

"Where do you fit in there?"

"Anywhere I want to."

I got off the phone with her, headed over, and sat down on a bench in front of the cathedral, next to a man with a giant python snake. A street performer had just finished his act, and a cop walked over and arrested him.

The performer kept saying indignantly, "Officer, why are you doing this?" over and over and "I am not resisting arrest." He then tried to appeal to the people, saying, "Ladies and Gentlemen! Ladies and Gentlemen! I'm being arrested for performing the show! Please! Ladies and Gentlemen! I need a witness!"

Some woman approached the handcuffed performer and stuffed her card into his pocket. The officer told her to walk away immediately or she would be arrested for obstructing justice. She rolled her eyes and slowly walked off.

"Antonio! Antonio!" the performer yelled as he saw another performer he knew. Antonio came over and the performer handed him a phone number and asked him to call it.

The cop car arrived and as they started putting him into it, Antonio yelled over to him that there was no answer.

The performer kept yelling (desperately and/or dramatically), "Try again! Try again!" The cops loaded his equipment into the trunk, and they drove off.

The man with the python turned to me and said, "Yeah, with all the vice going on in this town, you'd think the cops might have something better to do than arrest a street performer."

"What did they arrest him for?" I asked, making sure that his python's head wasn't heading in my direction.

"Oh he probably didn't have a permit, or something else life-or-death like that."

At that point, some girl walked over and wanted her picture taken with the python, so I said goodbye and got up.

I was in the mood to see some greenery, some grass, something living, something other than concrete, so I went inside the gate and walked along the sidewalk surrounding the statue of Andrew Jackson. That was my labyrinth. Other than the river, that was as close as I usually got to nature in the Quarter. Although some of the courtyards were beautiful and lush with greenery, there was still a lot of pavement. Some days I just needed to walk on grass.

There were often homeless alcoholic men sitting on a bench in the inner sanctum of the Square, but to the best of my knowledge, they were harmless, and they'd often just smile and tell me, "Hi." Some of them were probably just boozers, but others were undoubtedly old souls.

I left there and crossed Decatur at the traffic light by Jax Brewery. In the little park under the floodwall, a well-dressed woman was giving haircuts to homeless people.

I watched for a minute, then headed up to the river and sat on a bench. There were often some homeless up there as well, but again, they seemed harmless and never gave me any trouble.

Some man came and sat on the other end of my bench. We started talking, and he told me that he was homeless by circumstance and only temporarily, that he worked odd jobs during the day, building platforms and such, but that he was leaving in a few days to go work offshore, and then he'd be able to get back on his feet.

I noticed he had a fresh haircut. I asked him about the woman I had just seen cutting hair. He said, "Yeah, apparently that woman is a hairdresser in a salon, but she comes over here and gives free haircuts on a regular basis. It really helps out a lot because if one of us wants to go get a job, it makes it that much easier."

It turned out that he was a college-educated homeless person and had majored in English, so we somehow got into a discussion about the writings of D.H. Lawrence and how they had influenced the Beatnik Movement, which, in turn, led to the political movements and uprisings of the 1960's.

After he left, I sat staring out at the river for a while. A tugboat went by, and I had one of my *what-if* daydreams. I imagined what it would be like if I swam out to the tugboat with nothing but the clothes on my back, asked them to take me wherever they were going, and wherever that was, I'd survive and live there somehow.

Then the thought crossed my mind that it was probably that type of experience that a lot of the original European immigrants to New Orleans had had. I got up and headed home, to the home I had made in this strange land.

I often had what-if daydreams. Most of them were just diversions, a way to experience more things than I'd ever have the chance to actually get around to doing. But if the daydream were good enough, I'd follow it—like the one that had brought me to New Orleans in the first place.

7

Purple, Green, and Gold

Some tourists mistakenly assume that every place on Bourbon Street is sleazy and degenerate year-round. So naturally, some assumed that our club was sleazy too. Most of the time, they were wrong. Most of the time, we were a respectable establishment. Most of the time, it wasn't Mardi Gras.

Usually we attracted genuine blues lovers, other musicians (famous and otherwise), and tourists who just happened to wander in because they liked the sound. We normally didn't accommodate the local or visiting prostitutes, and the managers normally didn't tolerate a great deal of real sleazy behavior in our club.

But as Mardi Gras approached, everything got so crazy that it was hard to restrain, so we let almost everything slide other than the two greatest offenses: fighting and not paying the bill. Everything else was pretty much *anything goes*.

I won't go into the wanton depravity the entire week before Mardi Gras, but I will say that at first, it seemed fun and maybe almost even cute, but that it quickly deteriorated into an annoying hysteria.

Working during Mardi Gras was difficult, unpleasant, and definitely not financially rewarding. There were so many people in the club that we could barely walk through, but very few were tipping. They were too cheap or too drunk to remember or care about things like that.

Then, after hours of wading through the madness, when we'd finally get off and want nothing more than to go home, it would take an hour or two just to walk a few blocks because the mob on the street was jam-packed shoulder-to-shoulder, maybe closer, and they were hardly moving, and would actually come to a dead stand-still every time someone on a balcony would either flash breasts, or conversely, toss beads down to someone in the crowd who was flashing breasts. That took place at almost every balcony, so we were having almost minus movement, sometimes actually even moving backward. For people like me who had just gotten off a long shift at work, it was like, "Aw, come on! Not again!"

What I did enjoy though was walking around the Quarter in the daytime during Mardi Gras. It was even more colorful than usual, yet the crowd wasn't as intense and overwhelming as it was at night.

Someone had told me that purple, green, and gold, the colors of Mardi Gras, represent justice, faith, and power. Justice, faith, and power? I didn't see it. Maybe buried somewhere deep in the history of it. As the excitement mounted, all I saw were people out to celebrate, to convert, or to cash in.

On my way to the A&P grocery Saturday afternoon, I saw a flock of bald-headed Hari Krishna's singing, clapping, and jingling bells as they walked down the sidewalk on Royal Street. They all looked so peaceful and happy. Not that being in a cult appealed to me in any way, but they did give off that appearance.

When I got to the grocery, the narrow aisles were way too crowded for me to feel like or even tolerate shopping. I decided I could survive off deli food for a few days, as I carefully eased my way out of the store.

I left there and headed over to Jackson Square. The regulars were around, but there were also a lot of travelers out there working. Nomadic merchants were selling jewelry, beads, and various other items. There were a few people doing face painting. Others were braiding hair and letting the customer choose the colors of string that they'd intertwine in the braid.

There were jugglers performing various feats; some acts included acrobatics and swallowing fire. Yep, swallowing fire. That was kind of impressive.

Local Street Musicians were out, as well as some groups that just seemed to be passing through with Carnival. Jazz bands with musicians ranging from grammar-school age to grandparent age were also playing in various locations. Horns. There were lots of horns.

There were Painters/Artists/Caricaturists, and some of them were entertainers as well. There was a man from Mexico painting with cans of spray paint. Watching him quickly create a painting in moments was a show in itself, possibly even better than the finished product, and a crowd was gathering around him to watch. Music in the background added to the drama.

There were Mimes and Pantomimes. One Mime/Musician had a sign that said, "Sax Machine. What you drop is what you get." When someone would drop a tip in his case, he'd become a musician and play saxophone.

Throughout the French Quarter, musicians, artists, and entrepreneurs were working the streets. I saw some people making their money by panhandling. They'd just walk up to people and ask for money, or sit next to a sign with some kind of creative message on it. One said, "Accepting donations for Booze. Please be generous."

I thought about heading over to the river, but stopped on Decatur Street because the Mardi Gras Indians were parading there.

They were wearing were some of the most elaborate costumes I had ever seen. Someone had told me that they make the costumes themselves, and they start making them the day after Mardi Gras—for the next year. It definitely looked as if it could take that long to sew all those beads on themselves. They were exquisite.

I fell into rhythm some with the drumbeats and tambourines, but then I had to leave to get ready for work.

That night was as claustrophobic and wild as the night before. After work, I managed to make it through the crowd to Michael's club, just as he was getting off. He kissed me on the cheek and said, "Hello sweetheart. You ready to go home?"

"You?"

"Definitely."

On the way, I told him about the night. He said, "Typical Mardi Gras stuff. Get ready because it will only get worse. That's why I want to go home now: to rest up and prepare myself."

"For what?"

"A great big Dionysian/Bacchus binge that's only just begun. You'll see."

He was right. Sunday night was also insane. Just more of the same really, including even more drunk people, more noise, more spilled drinks, and less breathing room.

After work, several of us headed over to Nugent's. I told Erica, "I honestly didn't know that many people could fit inside the club."

She rolled her eyes and said, "I know. If the Fire Marshall had come in, surely there would've been violations."

I asked the bartender to bring us a round, then said, "I don't see how people can like Mardi Gras or think it's a good thing."

"Oh Samantha, that's because you've been working through all of it. Wow! I completely forgot this was your first Mardi Gras. Have you even been to a parade yet?"

"Just part of the Indian one. None of the others have meshed with my schedule."

"Oh honey, you have to go to a parade—then you'll know."

"I'm scheduled to work tomorrow and Tuesday."

"Oh no. Absolutely not! I refuse to let you. See that new girl who worked Jennifer's station tonight? She wants to pick up shifts those days. You're going to give them to her and hang with me."

"Sounds good."

"It gets better. We're gonna do the VIP thing tomorrow. You know what? I'm not even gonna tell you. Just meet me at three at my place."

When I met her the next day, we caught a cab uptown to a two-story white colonial on St. Charles. There was a balcony on the second floor with some people on it. And several people were hanging around the front yard under the beautiful mossy trees.

I looked at Erica. She shrugged and said, "It's my uncle's place. I'm glad you're here to keep me company. Come on. Let's go in and check out the refreshments."

Inside, there was gumbo, jambalaya, and a fully-stocked bar with a man in a tuxedo serving drinks. Her uncle came over, kissed cheeks, and told us to help ourselves to anything we wanted.

We got drinks, went upstairs, and sat in some chairs on the balcony. Erica said, "There are two parades today: Proteus and Orpheus. We have some time to hang out here before they start."

"Good. You can give me the full Jake update."

She put her head down, then looked back up at me and said, "He wants to move in with me."

I laughed. "Well of course he does! Your place is gorgeous. I'd like to move in with you too."

She continued, saying, "He's kind of *between*. It's either this or Mama's."

"Hello Mama!"

"I'm thinking maybe just temporary?"

"I thought we had definitely decided that one of us should learn from my mistakes."

"Looks like it's going to have to be you."

"Oh great . . . . Hey! If I can shake Michael loose, can I move in with you too? I could have your other bedroom."

She laughed and said, "If you can shake Michael loose, you can go to the Moon."

We went down for more refreshments, then mingled out on the lawn. Most of the people there were decked in expensive feathers and beads. We didn't start out with any, but people walking by kept stopping to put some on us. More kissing cheeks and cheers.

Around five, some of the people started gravitating over to the gate to go out on the street and join the commoners for Proteus—my first parade. A couple minutes into it, two guys came over and put Erica and I up on their shoulders. It was really cool. Not only did we have a great view up there, we also got better beads and didn't have to bump into people or scramble on the concrete for them.

We stayed out there for the Orpheus parade too, then headed back through the VIP gates. The guys wanted to go with us, but we told them that we had boyfriends. They didn't think that was a good enough reason, so Erica gave them another: "Thanks, but not interested."

We got drinks and sat back up on the balcony. I asked, "So, is tomorrow more of the same?"

"Pretty much, only better. I won't be here though—I'll be at my brother's in Metairie. He's on their parade route too. You wanna come?"

"Thanks, but I'm hanging with Michael tomorrow. He's got an early gig; then we're supposed to hook up around one."

"Well, if you get a chance, step out a little earlier, or you'll miss most of it."

"All right, I think I will."

"The best is the Zulu parade at eight."

"In the morning!"

Erica smiled. "You only have to wake up that early once a year—for Mardi Gras. Then, everything's over by mid-afternoon. And everything is completely dead tomorrow night. That's the time to sleep."

"All right. Zulu at eight. I'll try."

"If you make it, try to catch a coconut."

"A real coconut?"

"I don't know, but it's all decorated. The Zulus hand them out. It's special to get one because they usually only hand them out to relatives or people they know well. But this year, the bass player in our blues band is riding with that float. Keep an eye out for him because if he sees you, he might hand you one."

"Okay, but I'll just give him a wave. I won't beg; I refuse to beg."

Michael woke me up the next morning: Fat Tuesday, the biggest day of the whole Mardi Gras season, on his way out the door. He told me what time his gig ended, and we picked a rendezvous place to hook up.

After he left, I jumped out of bed. It felt like Christmas. I finally understood why people get so excited about Mardi Gras. I decided I wanted to fully participate in the day, and to see and do and cover as much ground as I could.

I walked from my apartment all the way to Lee Circle, just in time to catch the Zulu parade. Some guy put me up on his shoulders, and when the bass player came by, he did hand me a coconut. It was very exciting at the moment, and everyone around me was extremely impressed; however, I later traded the coconut for a drink at Fat Harry's. It's not a choice I would have made sober, but by that time, I wasn't sober.

Throughout the day, I also caught about thirty cups, an umbrella, a spear, some key chains, doubloons, and some black lace panties.

I had to be fairly aggressive to obtain such a large assortment of cheap plastic, painted baubles, and tacky polyester; however, it all seemed quite worthwhile and necessary at the time. Oh and beg? I think I might have even begged . . . .

In addition to lots and lots of beads, people were wearing all kinds of costumes. I saw cavemen, people in togas, and even politicians and pop stars. The most innovative were the astronauts—four guys in white flight suits pushing a makeshift rocket around. The rocket was about six feet high and about three feet wide. It had walls, but no floor, so whenever one of the guys had to relieve himself, he just stepped inside the rocket—their own personal rolling port-a-potty.

Throughout the day, I saw some people I knew, but no Michael! Not at the rendezvous point, not at the rendezvous time, not at all. He wasn't there, we didn't hook up, and there was no finding him. I hate to say that he stood me up, but it definitely looked that way. It felt that way too.

When I finally got my drunken-self home to find that he still wasn't there, I went to an apartment across the street where they were having a party. Tony, from the laundromat, had told me about it.

Some guy wearing feathers, high heels, and lots of long beads answered the door. He was the most scantily clad person there, although there were several men in sequined bikinis. And there were more people wearing tiaras than I had ever seen in one room before.

Tony sashayed over to me, looking like Cinderella. After complimenting his outfit, I told him, "I never felt so under-costumed in my life!"

He looked me up and down and said, "Don't be embarrassed, Sister Woman! We'll have you decorated in no time."

He and a few friends took me back into the bedroom and dressed me up in costume. When we went back out, they presented me to everyone as Queen Neptune, whoever that is. Anyway, they made me feel fabulous. It was such a happy party, and I was having such a good time that I actually forgot about Michael for a sweet little while.

After I decided I'd had enough fun, I went back across the street to my apartment. Michael still wasn't there, but he finally stumbled in a little while later with some weak excuse for standing me up, which I chose to accept. He didn't even ask me why I had purple, green, and gold lame' wrapped all around my body. He just unwrapped me and hung the lame' on a guitar he had hanging on the wall.

After some mad passion, we slept through most of the next day, which was all right because we both had the night off.

When we got up, we debated whether we wanted to go out to obtain food, or order in. For living in New Orleans, we weren't really into the whole culinary cuisine thing. Food was a function required by the body, and eating it was something that enabled us to drink more and drink longer. Beyond that, we weren't too particular. We often ate in bars that also served food. In that way, we were able to consume two birds with one stone. Occasionally, one of us would cook, but not often enough that we could have survived off it.

We decided to stay home, order Mama Rosa's pizza, and watch an old black and white movie on our old black and white TV. That TV was the only thing old-fashioned about us. Lying on the floor in front of it, waiting for the pizza, Michael turned to me and said, "Maybe I'd cook more often if we had a bigger kitchen."

I lifted my foot up to the TV, turned the volume down with my toes, and said, "Maybe I'd cook more if there were more hours in the day. Maybe I'd even learn how to draw, or play piano, or levitate. I'd like to learn how to stretch and manipulate time for my benefit, but since I haven't learned how to do that yet, I have to make choices."

He propped up on one elbow and said, "I know what you mean. With the twenty-four hours that I currently have in a day, I already find it impossible to do everything I want to do.

I sat up and said, "Yeah, if I had to cook and clean the kitchen everyday, I might not have time to sit in Jackson Square and people-watch, or go to the river and philosophize with bums, or dance at festivals."

"I might not have time to practice my music or go check out other musicians to see what they're doing."

The pizza came. I paid for it and put it on the coffee table. As I opened it up and took a piece, I said, "We have to stay focused and keep our priorities straight and not wear ourselves out with domestic duties. Granted, there's nothing wrong with all that, but we shouldn't fool ourselves into believing that type of life is for us."

Michael reached for a slice, saying, "I know. A studio apartment is about all the cleaning I ever want to do. I'd only want a big house if I had someone else to dust it."

I closed the box and said, "Ah hell, I don't even want a big house. All I need is a closet of my own, and maybe I don't even need that."

The movie we were watching ended around midnight. Michael turned the TV off and asked, "Hey, you wanna go to CheckPoint Charlie's to hang out? We could even wash a few clothes."

"CheckPoint Charlie's? What's that? A laundromat?"

"No, it's a club with washers and dryers in it."

"You're kidding. That's like a dream come true."

"No. Not kidding. You have to see it."

We threw a few dirty clothes in a bag and caught a cab over there. It was the ultimate layout and a genius idea. Not only were there washers and dryers, there was also a fully-stocked bar, a live band, some pool tables, a TV, chairs and couches, and even some bookshelves filled with miscellaneous books.

A skinny guy wearing a mini-skirt and pigtails was bartending. He kept prancing around saying, "Cocktails, cigarettes, French fries?" in a sing-song voice. It was definitely worth the cab ride over there to do our laundry in such an entertaining place. Laundry . . . New Orleans style.

8
Poetry, Music, and Money

I was off the next night too, so after Michael left for his gig, I headed over to Josephine's. It was Josie's night off, but I still wanted to go there. It felt more like home than my apartment did.

I had just pulled out my notebook and started writing, when a man sat down next to me at the bar. His hair was long and brown and looked as if he hadn't brushed it in a long time. He looked clean though; he actually smelled like soap. He was ten or twenty years older than me and had sort of a timeless face.

He asked me, "Are you a writer, or are you just dashing off a letter?"

I smiled and told him, "I'm always writing something."

He reached his hand out to me and said, "Yeah, I knew you were a writer. My name is Matt. Let me buy you a drink." I shook his hand, told him my name, and ordered my vodka and water. He ordered a shot of Southern Comfort.

The bartender told him, "Easy Matt. That's Michael's girlfriend."

Matt looked over at me and smiled, then looked back at the bartender and said, "That's all right. She's my friend."

The bartender shrugged, tossed the bottles up, spun them in the air, and poured them both at once, one with each hand, then placed them in front of us. There was no need for the speed and the showmanship—there was only one other customer in there besides us, but he was showing off and having a little fun.

Matt paid him money and a compliment, then turned to me and said, "It's the act of writing itself that takes me to the other side. I find it necessary not only to live my life, but also to express myself in it on an almost constant basis."

I smiled and said, "I know what you mean. I spend half my life living it, and the other half documenting my impressions."

"Me too. I mostly write poems though."

"I write poems too, but I always have trouble ending them. I start lots of them though. I have one I just started right here."

"Can I hear it?"

"I just have one line so far: *I'd like to kiss the stars that bathe my eyes in light.*"

"Let me see the pen for a minute." He sat there thinking, then wrote, "*The Moon may be my Mother; I'm a Child of the Night.*"

We went back and forth like that for a little while. After filling a few pages, I said, "From now on, you can be my writing partner. You're good at looking at my stuff and throwing a quick, light ending on it."

I read one of our short ones to the bartender, and he liked it enough to buy us each a shot of Jagermeister.

I met up with Michael later and told him about Matt. He said, "Oh I know him. He's been around for a while. I think he may be asexual. I've never seen him with anybody. He's harmless though."

I didn't think Matt was asexual, but I didn't really know, and it didn't even matter. All I cared about was that

Michael didn't seem to mind me being friends with him. I was glad. I liked Matt.

The next night, Michael and I were getting ready to go to some cool new little gig he was trying out. I got dressed and asked him if the outfit I was wearing was appropriate. He looked me up and down, grinned, and said, "I was appropriate once—I didn't like it!"

I laughed and said, "You know, you're right. To hell with appropriate!"

We went to the bar where he was playing that night, solo for a change, and I ordered water and tipped the bartender for it. I really didn't need any alcohol, and the water was so incredibly refreshing.

He went up on stage and started performing. Since it was a one-man show, he just sat on a stool the entire time, played guitar, and sang. Still, it was enough for me. Maybe I even liked it better. Maybe I was the biggest groupie of all. Even though there were other people there, it felt like he was just singing to me.

We went straight home afterward. Michael brushed my hair, then held me and sang me to sleep. Sometimes he could be so sweet.

The next day, the magic of the music temporarily faded, and the reality of supporting a musician lover returned. Michael and I headed over to Werleins to get some guitar strings and picks. While we were in there, I saw some other patrons of the arts: girlfriends opening their purses to make purchases for their otherwise would-be starving musician boyfriends. I wasn't unique. That seemed to be the norm. Well, just until their next big gig, or until they got discovered, or *made it*, or whatever. Then it would all come back to us, and more. Yeah right. No breath-holding there. But we loved them, and we believed in them—what else could we do?

I went in to work that night to earn us some more income. That night was particularly slow, so we were all just standing around talking.

I said, "The tips here aren't fabulous, but they're usually enough for us girls to support ourselves, our musician and/or loser boyfriends, and our alcohol habit."

Jennifer said, "Speaking of loser, my boyfriend is sort of between jobs, and I'm barely pulling us through. I'm thinking about doing something desperate. Maybe I'll get bangs and a padded bra."

Erica looked at her and said, "Don't bother. I have bangs, and I don't need a padded bra, but I haven't made any money either."

With a straight face Dana added, "Just think, I could be home, drunk and crying, right now." She looked like she meant it too, and not only that, she looked as if that might be preferable. Kids were spending money on drink-after-expensive-drink, but not tipping.

Katie joined in, saying, "I wish they'd all go back to Pat O'Brien's where they came from," referring to a tourist spot where unsuspecting amateurs with low tolerance levels can get drunk relatively cheaply on one or two hurricanes.

We had a one-drink minimum, and the price of the entertainment was rolled into the drink price. After spending more money than they had anticipated for a beer at our club, the customers either couldn't afford to—or didn't feel like—tipping. They obviously hadn't come in because they were huge blues lovers. They seemed to have wandered in by mistake.

By 12:30 A.M., all Dana and Katie had in their tip jar from the entire night was four dollars, so Dana walked over to the deli, exchanged the sum for lottery tickets, and won twenty dollars. We thought that was so enterprising. Erica, Jennifer and I decided to try the same thing. We each contributed a dollar. Jennifer went and bought us a ticket, but we didn't have the same luck. It just made us each a dollar poorer.

While we were hanging around, I asked Erica if Jake had moved in yet.

She grinned and said, "No, he found a friend he could stay with."

"You know that's a good thing, right?"

"Oh definitely." She sighed and added, "These men. They're just hard to turn down sometime."

"I know how that is. There are times that Michael would probably be homeless if it weren't for me, or somebody like me. But lucky for him, there are people just like me, lined up behind me."

During the band's last set for the night, some homeless man came in and sat down at a table. Roger marched over to him—almost before he even sat down—and told him that he was going to have to leave. The man got mad, threw the brown bag he was carrying down onto the floor, and stormed out.

I picked the bag up, opened it, and looked inside. It had a fresh banana and an apple in it. I thought it was so strange that he left it behind. I raced over to the door and looked out, trying to catch him, but he was already gone. I set it on the sidewalk right outside the door.

Roger came over and said, "I first met that man two years ago. He told me he was a millionaire movie producer from California."

"Was he?"

"I don't know. He didn't look like a bum then. He started out in a suit and tie, with a good haircut. He said he was giving it all up for a little while so that he could do research for a book on homeless people. Unfortunately, he got caught up in the Mad Dog 20/20 and the street life and quickly went downhill."

"A lot of people do that: they come here for one reason and end up forgetting what it was."

"I guess that's what happened to him. Either that or he's really into his research."

Other than that man's bag of fruit, all I found on the floor that night was a five-dollar bill, which was, of course, better than nothing. We always made a point of searching around for money, especially under the chairs and barstools. That might as well have been part of our job description or an included part of our salary: low base, plus tips, plus whatever we could scrounge off the floor.

Sometimes we'd get lucky and find a twenty or two. Super Bowl weekend, Erica found three fifty-dollar bills. Once, Katie found five-hundred dollars all in one bundle. She said she was shaking. Tourists would get so drunk and careless; it was inevitable that some of them would drop some money occasionally.

Of course the fact that it was so dark in the club helped our cause. At the end of the night when everyone would clear out and the manager would turn the light on, we'd all quickly scan the floor for our last chance of the night to find some money. We always turned valuables in, but there wasn't a Lost and Found for cash. When found loose, not contained in a wallet or purse, it was always Finders-Keepers.

It was Katie's Birthday, so we headed over to Nugent's to celebrate. At some point, there was an empty seat next to her at the bar, so I sat down and bought her a drink. She was telling me about her night; then somehow we got into a discussion about what it's like being the girlfriend of a musician.

Suddenly inspired, I proclaimed, "We ought to start our own band and call it 'Girlfriend's Revenge'."

She looked at me as if I were brilliant and said, "We should! Do you play any musical instruments?"

"No."

"Me neither."

"Oh well, we'll worry about that later on."

"Hey, we could get Erica in on this too now."

"Definitely."

Around that time, her boyfriend, Danny, stumbled over. He and Katie tried to decide who was sober enough to drive since he had recently gotten a DUI. I guess they figured it out because they said their goodbyes and left.

In the meantime, Michael had arrived, and having caught the end of the conversation, he turned to me and slurred, "I never actually explained to you what it is to *be* a Musician . . . ."

I thought to myself, *Oh no! Not again! Only a thousand different times in a thousand different ways.*

Outwardly, I prepared myself for another one of his long-winded monologues. I'd have to come up with something else to think about while I maintained eye contact with him and nodded every once in a while, pretending to listen. Either that or I'd have to try to fight the urge to bang my head against the bar while actually listening to him. I loved him dearly, but sometimes he could be so dull.

9
VIP's at Tip's and the FQ Fest

The next night, Michael and I headed uptown to Tipitina's, via a couple of streetcars. We were quiet on the way over there, just looking out the windows. I loved the elegant old garden district homes, again with the hanging ferns, and the moss hanging off the stately trees. I always thought that when I got rich, I'd buy one of those houses like Anne Rice did. Ah—to write of New Orleans and live well—what could be better than that?

We were on the guest list at Tip's because Michael knew the lead guitarist. We were on the list every time we went there because Michael would either know someone in the main band or the opening band, or else we wouldn't go. Still, it was always exciting standing there while they checked for our names.

When we walked in, I headed straight for the bathroom and got in line behind a few other people.

A girl came stumbling out of one of the stalls and said, "Y'all, you don't want to go in there; I just barfed my brains out."

"Are you all right?"

"Yeah, but does anyone have some breath mints or some gum or something? I don't want my date to know I puked."

"No, sorry."

Someone volunteered, "Hey, why don't you try gargling with Spearmint Schnapps. That usually works."

"Thanks, I'll try that."

Ah, the college life. Fall had come and gone, and I hadn't returned to school, but I remembered what it was like.

The show was entertaining, and so was the audience. We alternated between dancing in front of the stage with the wild people and watching the show from the balcony upstairs with the slightly more sophisticated mellowed crowd. Downstairs was a little more our scene.

Afterward, we hung out with the band in the VIP room. It was nothing fancy, just some tables and chairs and messy writing on the walls. I guess it was the exclusive aspect that made it special . . . that and the free food and booze.

Refreshments consisted of three large Domino's pizzas, a platter of cheese and crackers, an untouched vegetable platter, a big bowl of fruit—also untouched, and a box of Popeye's chicken, which was, by far, the most popular item. There was also an extra large ice chest full of bottled beer (Rolling Rock and Dixie Voodoo), several bottles of liquor (quite a few still unopened), and a bottle of Champagne, which we immediately opened and drank. It was a decent bottle, and I guess it made us feel even a little more VIP.

After hanging out there for about an hour, Michael and I invited the ten or so remaining people over to our place. We grabbed a full bottle of tequila on the way out and piled into the drummer's van.

Back at our apartment, Michael passed shot glasses around to everyone for the tequila. I was rather intoxicated at that point and opted for a bottle of water. It was a wise choice, but would have been even wiser a little earlier.

It seemed like a cool get-together. I remember wondering *Why don't we do this more often?* Then one of our guests leaned forward and puked on the carpet with no warning. *Oh yeah, that's why.* Fortunately, I passed out around that time, so Michael had the unpleasant job of cleaning up all the half-digested pizza chunks. He probably did a better job than I would have anyway. I was certainly no domestic goddess.

The next day I awoke to shot glasses and disarray, but at least all the people were gone, including Michael. He had already left for an early gig. I looked around and decided to leave everything as it was. We could worry about it later on, or not . . . whatever.

Anyway, I really wanted to go to the French Quarter Festival. I called Erica to see if she wanted to go with me.

She said, "No, I have to do laundry, and I'm probably gonna be late for work as it is."

"Yeah, I have to work tonight too, but I'm gonna go over and hang out for a little while."

"You don't mind going by yourself?"

"No. I go to festivals by myself a lot actually. Michael goes with me sometimes, but most of the time, he has a gig, or we're fighting or something, so I just go solo. I don't care. I always have fun."

I started out over at Jackson Square. They had several food booths set up, serving an assortment of entrees and appetizers: crawfish etoufee', crawfish remoulade, crawfish pie, crawfish-whatever-you-want, shrimp Creole, barbeque ribs, Italian sausage in marinara on bread, etc. I opted for gumbo.

They were also serving beer in souvenir cups. All the festivals sold beer, and I'd always buy it. Some people said the beer was overpriced, but actually it was just priced at what the market would bear. I was the market, and I was willing to bear it. Although I drank vodka in bars or at night, sometimes I liked to have a beer or two during the day. That was my version of a soft drink.

The most important attraction of any festival for me, however, was always the music. It being a New Orleans festival, there was fabulous live entertainment, of course. New Orleans musicians make everything sound at least a little bit funky, and I mean that only in the most enthusiastically flattering way. I saw Germain Basil at

Jackson Square and Charmaine Neville at Woldenberg Park. Needless to say, there was a lot of dancing.

Most of the time at festivals, I'd dance by myself. I didn't care. A lot of other people did it too. Inevitably, some guy would come over and try to dance next to me, usually someone I'd have absolutely no interest in under any circumstances. I'd just try to ignore him.

There was one old man, though, that went to most of the festivals, and he'd always dance by himself too, so I started dancing next to him whenever I'd see him. He didn't mind, and that way, the young guys would leave me alone. He reminded me of my grandfather. Something about his demeanor and personality was the same. He just seemed familiar, and I felt comfortable near him, even though we never really talked, just danced alongside one another. It was a genderless, ageless, free-spirited dance.

I reluctantly left there and headed over to work. It started pouring down rain on the way, so when I walked in the door, I was dripping wet. Katie took one look at me and said, "What, no umbrella?"

I smiled and told her, "I love walking to work in the rain with no umbrella, dodging lightning bolts the whole way, all the men standing in the doorways telling me, 'You're gonna catch a cold, dawlin.' I never do."

Katie just smiled at me as if she knew I'd say that, then walked off.

After I dried off a little, a group of tourists came in wearing plastic rain ponchos with the words "Bourbon Street" printed all over. If we hadn't known they were tourists anyway, that would've been a dead giveaway. I turned and saw them approaching just as they walked by and slimed me on the arm with their wet ponchos. *Ick! Poncho Juice!*

Erica slipped in behind them. She was late, but Roger didn't notice.

A little while later the club owner came in, high on Ecstasy. Erica said, "Oh well, it's good to see him happy once in a while, even if it is artificially induced."

I asked her, "Have you ever done Ecstasy?"

"I tried it once, but I know some people who took it way too many times and it seemed to make them crazy, possibly even did some permanent neurological damage, so I never took it again."

"I'll pass on the permanent neurological damage."

"Yeah, me too. I'm just slowly working my way to wet brain."

I laughed and said, "Slow is the way to go."

Before leaving, the owner gave us all drinks "on the house," not that we wouldn't have taken them anyway. Still, we appreciated the gesture.

By the end of the night, there was rain and mud everywhere, inside and outside. On my way home from work, I ran into a guy I knew, sloshing down the thunderstorm-soaked street. He told me he was on his way to return a girl's Harley Davidson bikini underwear that he had obtained while drinking at Johnny White's the night before and claimed, "Such is the life of a single man!"

When I got home, I didn't have a soul to talk to. Of course, I could have gone out after work, but I'd had enough humidity for one night, and besides, I thought Michael was going to be up. He had called me at work and asked me to bring him a bourbon and coke. Since I thought he'd be waiting up, I rushed home, not with a bourbon and coke, but with a monstrous shot of Jagermeister.

Although the jazz was still blasting from the stereo, the lights were out and Michael was dead asleep. I jumped up and down on the mattress a few times, laughing like a maniac, then rolled over him twice, you know, just trying to get his attention, but he appeared unmoved. I even kissed him on his paralytic lips several times before he managed to mutter a "Hey, babe," quickly followed by a snore. Guess he didn't really need a drink after all.

I leaned back against my pillow and drank the Jagermeister myself. It did its magic again. The mind-altering sensations, which rippled through, yet numbed me were all quite welcome—and they knew it.

Jagermeister . . . so smooth. Makes me wanna break a bathtub apart with my bare teeth, then pass out.

Actually, I did break someone's bathtub before—part of it anyway. I was attempting to sit on the toilet, missed, fell headfirst into the bathtub and broke the soap dish off with my head. Ever since that night, I had restricted my intake of Jagermeister, and no matter what, I never surpassed my quota. At least I don't think so. Not that I'm aware of anyway.

My college roommate's words from the past echoed through my mind: "Let the couch absorb you. The couch is your friend." Well, the room was absorbing me, millisecond by millisecond, until I looked over at Michael and remembered where I was and who I was. Although he was asleep, his mere presence calmed me and put me completely at ease. Adrift in subconsciousness, he didn't even realize it. Or maybe he did. Maybe we were drifting along together in parallel planes . . . .

10
Sax on the Roof

On my birthday, I discovered my first gray hair while primping in front of the bathroom mirror. I showed it to Michael and asked, "Does this mean I'm a woman now?"

He picked me up, spun me around and said, "Only in the best way, darling! Let's go celebrate."

We headed over to a festival taking place nearby. On the way, I asked him, "Do you think I could halt the aging process through positive thinking and self-hypnosis?"

"Who knows? Anything's possible."

When we arrived, Paul Prudhomme was zipping around on his cart. I got my picture taken with him, and danced with Oliver "Who Shot the La La" Morgan. I felt like such a local.

We left around sunset, got some champagne at the deli, and took it home. I put the feather boa around my neck, put a black hat on Michael, and we danced around laughing. Then we took the champagne and climbed out our French windows onto the roof.

Michael told me, "Stay right here," ducked inside, and came back with his saxophone. The guitar was more his forte. He wasn't brilliant with a sax, but he tinkered with it now and then, and he knew a few songs quite well.

I poured us each a drink, and we toasted our fabulous selves. Then Michael played Louis Armstrong's "Do You Know What It Means to Miss New Orleans." I was exuberant! I love that song.

After he finished, I kissed him on the lips and told him, "It's times like this that I remember why I ever loved you in the first place."

He looked at me puzzled and said, "I always remember why I love you."

"Yeah, Michael, but it's not that exclusive kind of love that I'd be able to settle down to."

"I don't know what *exclusive* love means."

"My point exactly. But hey, let's not ruin a beautiful evening by talking nonsense. Have some champagne and play another song, would you?"

He did "Moon River" from the movie *Breakfast at Tiffany's* with Audrey Hepburn. It was perfect. It matched the mood; it matched the costume; it matched the night. After that, we saw fireworks over the river, and I think they may have been real too.

When I woke up the next day, Michael's eyes were already open. He was looking at me and smiling.

I smiled back and told him, "I just had a really vivid dream. I dreamed that I could fly. I was flying over the French Quarter and looking down at all the rooftops."

He rose up on an elbow and said, "Cool! Did you see ours?"

"I was looking for it, but I couldn't make it out because then I couldn't remember where I lived, or when I lived, or even who I was."

"I know what you mean. I've had dreams like that before, but then when I wake up, it's hard to relate it to my everyday life here."

"Yeah, every time I dream I'm flying, it's like I just remembered how to do it, and I can't believe how easy it is—or that I ever even forgot how."

He stretched and said, "A dream like that helps put everything in perspective."

"It helps me realize that I worry too much about stuff that doesn't matter."

"Which stuff is that—the stuff that doesn't matter?"

"I don't know. Maybe all of it."

"Like nothing means anything?"

"Or everything means something, but not what we think."

"Yeah, like what?"

I sat up. "Maybe we're not being graded. Maybe life is not a pass/fail exam. Maybe in the end we all pass, but some of us just choose to retake the test more often. Maybe it's not even a test. Maybe it's just a way to experience ourselves more than we did before."

He sat up too and said, "Maybe there is no end. Maybe *now* is all there is."

"Yes, but a bigger *now* than we could even begin to imagine, an eternal kind of *now* that includes everything. Like time as we know it doesn't even exist. It's an oversimplification."

He stood up, reached for my hand to pull me up, and said, "If *now* is all there is, I want to do something meaningful in it."

Since water is seemingly eternal and ageless, we decided to take a boat ride. Being broke, however, we didn't take one of the expensive boat rides that were mostly filled with tourists anyway. We took the free ferry ride to Algiers and back. We liked to ride it sometimes and pretend that we were on some foreign ocean, en route to some exotic country. This time we pretended we were just leaving Italy for Greece.

We often daydreamed that we were Bohemian vagabonds living off our talent and wit. He'd sing for his supper, and I would write prose and poetry. Our life would be a lyrical ballad with pretty sunsets and all. So lovely to dream about, so difficult to live.

At one point, we talked about the two of us going to Canada and riding the rails like hobos. Another time we talked about hitchhiking out to California and surviving out there somehow. Our most ambitious and adventurous plan was to start saving up for a backpacking trip across Europe.

The only glitch in any of these plans was that we could barely pay our rent each month and hadn't saved a dime.

Ah, but the dreaming was free. The dreaming was divine. It was reality that sometimes kicked us in the butt.

Dorothy Parker's words were so fitting and apropos:

> Oh life is an endless cycle of song,
> A medley of extemporanea.
> And love is a thing that can never go wrong,
> And I am Marie of Romania.

11
Typical Day

The next day, I had to go downtown to put money in the bank so I could pay my bills. It hadn't been a very good month at work, but the last week had been pretty good, so I at least had enough. Barely.

Anyway, although going to the bank may have been a typical mundane task for some, it usually wasn't for me. The first thing I had to do was locate my stash of cash. I had to keep it hidden from Michael, and I had to constantly change my hiding place. One time, he found the stash and spent most of it. We had to go a couple of days without electricity that month. We tried to make the best of it and pretend that it was romantic and intimate hanging out in the candlelight, but the fact remained—no electricity! Another time, he took my card without asking and tried to withdraw money, but he didn't know my password, so he kept trying different things until the ATM machine ate my card!

When he'd pull that kind of crap, I'd get really mad, he'd be really charming, and finally I'd forgive him. But I'd swear that my next boyfriend was going to be rich, boring, and predictable. Michael was none of those things.

After locating my cash, I headed out. Although I sometimes took the bus to the central business district, I really wasn't in the mood for it, so I decided to take a long walk there instead.

As I approached the corner of Dauphine and Conti, I saw a guy laughing, frowning, getting louder, getting quieter. Heard him saying, "There was a little SPIDER who sat down BESIDE her and" (looking directly at me and pointing at me as I passed him, screaming at the top of his lungs), "YOU'LL BE ALL RIGHT if . . ." (Then he threw both his arms into the air screaming), "DRUGS! Sat on her Tuffeettttt."

I continued walking nonchalantly, but sped up slightly, glancing back occasionally to make sure he wasn't following me or bearing down on me with a huge knife or anything like that. Fortunately, he wasn't.

On Canal Street, I ran into a girl I had met when I first came to town, and I asked her how she was doing. She said, "Same old story—I need money!"

I told her, "I know what you mean. My life is a series of bills I can't pay and a list of things I won't get done today. Ah, but I trudge on through the madness anyway."

"Madness is right," she said. "I have no electricity, no water, no phone service, and I'm about to get evicted from my apartment."

I managed to fight back the urge to roll my eyes. It was the second or third time that had happened to her since I had known her. It was hard to feel sorry for her because she was beautiful, intelligent, and able-bodied. She just couldn't get it together because apparently, cocaine, weed, and alcohol came first before paying her bills.

Anyway, I was in no position to help her even if I wanted to, so she had to move on to find someone else who could. As she was walking away, I smiled and said, "I see you have your red lipstick on."

She smiled back and said, "I'm not as bad as some, but I'm worse than others." Then she winked at me, and walked on.

She had once told me that if she didn't have any food and only had two dollars to her name, she would spend that money on a tube of lipstick because then she could get a man to take her out to dinner in a nice restaurant. I thought that was so funny at the time. Nevertheless, she was starting to age, and she would reach a point where she needed a lot more help than a tube of lipstick.

A few minutes later, as I was walking down the street, a man asked, "What is your name?" Not realizing he was talking to me, I kept walking and didn't answer, so he got closer and repeated, "What is your name?"

I turned and told him, and right then, it dawned on me who he was: the homeless man I had discussed the Beatniks with at the river one day. He looked much gruffer than he had before, obviously homeless now. When I had first met him, he hadn't looked homeless because he kept himself groomed, showered at friend's places, and he'd even had that fresh haircut.

He told me, "I just got out of jail recently. Spent sixty days in there for fighting."

"You don't seem like the type to pick a fight. What happened?"

"It was self-defense. Me and about fifteen others got arrested on the corner of Magazine and Josephine. They tried to say it was a gang fight, but it wasn't."

"Well that sucks."

"Yeah, the worst part is that I lost my job while I was doing time. It really set me back. I might have a job coming up on the boat, but it's not until next week. I'm not suffering too bad, but I've definitely seen better days."

I told him I didn't have any money to spare, which was true, then wished him luck, and we went our separate ways.

I finally made it to the bank and made my deposit; then I walked back home down Bourbon Street. The Strip Club barkers were already out. One of the big burly ones, all slicked up in a suit and tie, looked me up and down and offered me a job. I smiled, gave him that *yeah, right* look, said, "No thank you," and kept walking.

As I passed Marie Laveau's House of Voodoo, I saw
tourists going in to buy the tee shirt showing that they had
been there. I wondered if there was anything to that voodoo
stuff. I think a lot of it is just a way to make money off the
tourists, like anything else in the Quarter. Still, it all seemed
kind of Wizard of Oz to me. Like somewhere, hidden
behind the curtain, there might be a real Wizard. The rest
was just flash, pomp, and circumstance.

It was dusk by then when I passed Lafitte's
Blacksmith Shop. I could see the glow of the fireplace and
the candles shining in the dimly-lit bar. The man wasn't
singing at the piano yet, but the jukebox was going. For
some reason, that jukebox seemed totally out of place to me
there. The piano fit.

One of the oldest bars in the United States, inside it, I
always felt as if I had gone back in time. I loved to go in
there sometimes, but it was the kind of place that I totally
had to be in the mood for. It had so much character,
history, and intrigue, but there was a little sadness in it too.
I couldn't go in there if I was depressed, but I didn't want to
go in if I was too upbeat either. It was a good place to go
when I was in a middle-of-the-road nostalgic mood.

Back to my apartment, home sweet whatever. I
poured myself a glass of wine, sat out on the roof, and
reflected on my day as I began my night. At least now I
knew the real version of Little Miss Muffett . . . .

I was off work, so I changed my outfit and headed out.
The manager at Michael's club-du-jour didn't allow
girlfriends to hang out there, so I went to the little bar
around the corner from his club.

As I walked in, a stripper from one of the local
burlesque clubs was pulling her right breast out to prove to
a guy at the bar how firm it was. She tucked it back in and
said, "Guys at work are always asking me if I'm a body
builder. I tell them, 'No, why?' They say, 'Because all the
other girls are so skinny.' I tell them, 'That's because they
all do cocaine, and I don't.'"

After that, she somehow managed to wrap her legs
around his neck, while he was standing. Then, she leaned

all the way back until she was upside down and started bending her knees and making erotic pelvic maneuvers.

After that demonstration, some guy tripping on acid came and sat down and started talking to me. After a couple of minutes, he told me, "You got good choice in make-up. You smell perty. See, your smile is so perty, it doesn't even matter what kind of conversation we're having. I don't even remember what we're talkin' about, and it doesn't even matter."

He walked off saying, "To fathom hell and soar angelic, just take a hit of psychedelic."

A few people at the bar were playing a dice game called Chicago. I played once. Five of us each put up a dollar. I won the round, so I got the money. If I were much of a gambler, I probably would have stayed and played some more. As it was, I was happy to collect my five bucks and move on. I had been there long enough to determine that it wasn't really my scene.

I left there and went to Josephine's, which was always my scene. It wasn't very lively either, but at least Josie was there. She had a Renaissance-festival look going on and even had a floral bouquet in her hair, with her braids pinned up underneath it.

After complimenting her outfit, I told her, "The night wasn't dead, just slow and weird."

She quickly added, "like most of our friends."

We both laughed. It was Friday night in the French Quarter but I could hardly feel a pulse. The heart was beating, but the flow was faint. I could hear a beat, I could feel the beat, but it was just the jukebox.

Matt floated in and perched on the barstool next to me. There was always an air of innocence about him. He was like a little bird who wasn't afraid of anything because, despite everything, he didn't believe in evil.

He ordered his usual: Southern Comfort. I started writing a poem on a beverage napkin and passed it over to him. It said:

> I live on the outskirts of town
> Where Southern Comfort
> Is the only comfort around
> Just me and my thoughts spinning round
> On the outskirts
> The outskirts of town

He got right into it, grabbed another bev nap, and wrote another verse; then I added one, and we went back and forth until it was probably about ten bev nap's long. We thought that it was our most brilliant collaboration yet and had several drinks to celebrate.

The next day, I remembered the masterpiece while I was still lying in bed and jumped up all excited to go read it.

Unfortunately, I didn't have it. All I could find was that first bev nap with the first verse. The rest of it was lost forever, thrown out with the bar trash, disintegrated into nothingness. I called Matt to make sure that he didn't have the rest, but he didn't even remember writing it.

Oh well, it's there somewhere in our memory cells, perhaps someday to be recalled—unless those were the cells that got eaten away by the alcohol.

12
Historical Tour

After I hung up with Matt, Michael walked in with our coffee and asked, "What's up for today?"

"I don't know, but I'm free all day, I'm off work tonight, and I'm open for anything."

"I'm off too! Let's get ready, and we'll find something to do."

I took my coffee and headed into the bathroom. Bare feet on the black and white tile floor. I paused to look in the mirror above the pedestal sink. Yes, the hair could use a wash. Someone had been blowing bubbles at Josephine's the night before, and I must've caught some of them with my head. After showering, I blow-dried my bangs, but decided to let the rest dry naturally.

As I turned the blow dryer off, Michael barged in, as he always did. I had attempted, on several occasions, to get him to knock first, but I finally realized that I was just wasting my breath. He was impossible to train.

He blurted out: "I found something for us to do. A friend of mine just called and invited us to go to Marcus Garvey Day at Armstrong Park. I told him, 'Yes,' because you said you were up for anything. He'll be here in thirty minutes."

"Sounds good to me. Which friend?"

"Herman, from my band."

"Is he still dating that waitress from your club?"

"No. He's a really nice guy and very interesting, but he's not really a relationship guy."

I laughed and said, "Like you are?" as he sat down on the toilet and watched me put on my makeup.

Herman buzzed a little later. We went and met him downstairs, then headed over to Armstrong Park.

When we got there, we walked all around first to see what was going on. There were various people checking in on the status of equality, with differing opinions.

There were also several different bands playing throughout the park: jazz, blues, hip hop, even rock. We sat down on the grass to listen to a local band that had just started up and Michael went to get us some drinks.

I said something about the variety of the music, and Herman told me, "Actually, any type of New Orleans music is appropriate here because it all started here."

"Here where?"

"Here at Armstrong Park . . . in a part of it called Congo Square. The slaves used to gather here on Sunday, and among other things, they created music. Later, the Congo Square music gave birth to Ragtime, which gave birth to Jazz, which gave birth to the Blues, which gave birth to Rock and Roll."

"What an interesting family tree."

"Yeah, and even though they each exist as their own unique art form, they are all interrelated somehow."

"Like it says in the Muddy Waters song: 'The blues had a baby and they named it rock and roll.'"

"Yeah, kinda like that."

"So what other types of things did they do in Congo Square?"

"Oh they played musical instruments, especially drums. And there was dancing, of course, to accompany the music. And some people said that voodoo ceremonies went on there as well, presided over by none other than our famous Marie Laveau."

"Oh I saw her . . ."

Herman interrupted, "You saw her?"

I smiled and continued on, "I saw her at the Wax Museum. Kind of creepy, but kind of cool too. What got me though, was look at how much infamy, power, and respect she had back in the 1800's as both a black person and a woman. I can't think of another woman who had that much power in that century."

"No. But New Orleans was a very unique place at that time. It was extremely different from the puritanical New England influence that spread over a lot of the United States. It was influenced more by the underdog here. In some ways, it was No Man's Land, but in other ways, anybody had a chance here. Women probably did have more power here than in other places."

"Other women besides Marie Laveau?"

"Yeah, although probably not as well-known as she was. But believe me, a lot of the prostitutes around the French Quarter had more power and independence than plantation wives in the rest of the continent. Not all of them, of course, but some of them did."

Off to the side, there were two people doing something that looked like a combination between martial arts and dance. A few minutes later, another guy went up and gracefully joined in while the first guy backed out. It almost looked as if the second guy had just cut in on a dance.

Henry said, "That's Capoeira. Have you ever seen it before?"

"No. It's fascinating though."

"It started in Brazil. The slaves there weren't allowed to practice martial arts, but they found a way to do it anyway. They disguised it in dance."

Michael had just come back with our drinks. He handed them to us and said, "Wow! That's amazing. They're doing really complex moves, but they make it look so easy."

I added, "Yeah, when I watch them, I feel totally drawn to what they're doing, and I feel like I want to go join in too, you know, cut in and be next. And I really feel as if I could do it too. My rational mind knows that's impossible— that it would take years of practice to do that as gracefully as they are—but my body seems to feel otherwise."

Henry smiled. "I have a friend who takes classes. It's a little too acrobatic for me though. But you can sign up anytime you want to, if you're interested in learning."

Michael looked at me. "I'll sign up if you will."

I laughed and said, "I've always wanted to study martial arts, but I think maybe we should start on a smaller scale. I'm sort of athletic in a not-against-it kind of way. Put it this way: I do a lot of walking, but I never took gymnastics."

Henry grinned. "I hear you. Tae Kwon Doe might suit you better. I know someone who teaches it on Canal Street. I don't have his phone number with me, but I can give it to Michael tomorrow night at our gig."

We threw our food remains into the trash, then headed out of the park. Just as we reached the corner, a horse and buggy came and pulled up right next to us. Herman looked up and smiled. "That's my brother, Quincy."

Quincy leaned over and asked, "Can I give y'all a ride somewhere?"

As Herman climbed up, he said, "Complimentary, I hope."

Quincy said, "Of course. You know I won't take your money."

Herman reached down for my hand and pulled me up in one strong move. Michael climbed in beside me.

Quincy took us down Rampart Street and weaved through parts of Burgundy and Dauphine, giving us a tour along the way. He pointed out various locations, and told us about prostitution in the 1800's. "Some of them were born into it. Their mama's were in the biz. Some were sold into it by a relative, or sometimes even by a stranger."

"What do you mean *sold into it*? Like slaves?"

"No. You have to understand something. Things were different then. Once a woman was ruined—as in not married, but not a virgin—she didn't have many choices anymore. So, all anyone who wanted to make money off her had to do was to get her ruined the first time—and it wasn't always with her permission. Or, a man might seduce her, promising to marry her, but then abandon her. Same result."

"Rough life for women."

"It really was . . . for some of them."

He pulled over to the side and asked, "Where do y'all want to go next?"

I said, "Let's see, we've covered Armstrong Park, Congo Square, the Brothels . . . . Are there any other must-see historical landmarks for uninformed locals like us?"

Herman said, "Oh, I know. Could you take us by Bourbon and Orleans?"

Quincy turned at the next corner and said, "The Quadroon Balls. Of course."

"Quadroon Balls?"

"Oh yes. There was a place in the French Quarter where, although women marketed their beauty, they were not prostitutes, and their lives were fairly smooth."

He stopped in front of the Bourbon Orleans Hotel, and I looked up at the balcony. For a millisecond, I felt as if I were up there looking down, feeling sad, very sad. Then, the next moment, I felt as if I were back in my body now, but I was still feeling this deep sorrow; I didn't know why.

Michael asked me, "Is something wrong?"

"No . . . . I just feel as if I've been in there before, but I don't think I have."

"Maybe you've been in another hotel that's similar?"

"Maybe . . . ."

Quincy looked back at Herman and said, "You can tell this one."

Herman leaned forward and said, "This is where the Quadroon Balls used to take place. In the 1800's—and even before, wealthy white men used to come to the Quadroon balls to meet certain Free Women of Color. Quadroon actually referred to a woman who was a quarter black, but there was a whole range. Octoroons were one-eighth black.

"After a man selected a woman, if she accepted, he would sometimes set her up in an arrangement that was almost like marriage. He'd buy her a little cottage in or near the French Quarter; then he'd provide for her and any children they might have together."

"Did he live there too?"

"No, but he'd spend a lot of time there. Sometimes that arrangement would end when he married a Caucasian woman . . . sometimes it wouldn't."

"So he might end up with two families: one light, one dark. But not legally a bigamist because he only took the marriage license out for one of them, right?"

"Yes, but the other arrangement was rather formal too and had its own rules and protocol. Contracts were often drawn up. It wasn't marriage, but it had a name. It was called placage."

We sat in silence for a moment, then Michael asked, "How about a ghost tour next?"

I shook my head. "Oh, I am definitely going to have to pass on that one."

Quincy said, "That's cool. It's about time for me to get back to work anyway. I can drop y'all off anywhere in the Quarter, then I'm heading back to Jackson Square to get some paying rides."

He dropped Michael and me off on our street. After thanking him, I said, "Hey, I work at The Blue. Do you have any business cards on you? I could pass them out to tourists at the club."

He said, "Thanks. I'd appreciate that," and handed some over.

"I will definitely recommend you."

Michael and I stopped at the deli on the corner to get some food to take back to our place. He ordered Shepherd's Pie. I asked him what it was.

"Oh, you get everything. It's got ground beef, mashed potatoes, peas."

I ordered a Chef Salad and said, "Oh look: I got everything too. It's just a different everything."

After we finished eating, the phone rang. It was a friend of Michael's asking him to fill in for him at his gig. Since we didn't have any other big plans, he accepted and headed over.

I did a little writing, then went to bed early—for a little while anyway. I had a strange dream. Well, I should say: my strange dream. I'd had it before, or variations of it. I was walking through the French Quarter at night, and as I got to the corner of Royal and Toulouse, I stopped and asked myself: *Isn't that where the A&P is supposed to be?*

Then I realized that other things were different too. It was very dark; there was no electricity, and there were no cars on the street. I realized it must be a different time period. I heard footsteps coming. I turned around, but before I could see the person, I woke up.

The dream had felt so real; I couldn't go back to sleep. I got dressed and started walking down Bourbon Street. As I was passing Johnny White's, I saw Dana sitting at the bar, so I went in, sat down next to her, and bought her a drink. She had been warming up to me lately. I was slowly starting to win her over with my charm. And besides, who turns down a drink?

I told her, "I went to bed at midnight—can you believe it? I can't remember the last time I went to bed so early."

She took a big sip and said, "Why that's almost suburban. Before we know it, you'll be married, cutting coupons, and moving out to the country."

"Highly doubtful. After going to bed at midnight, I woke up around two A.M. from a really strange dream. I couldn't get back to sleep, so I got dressed and came here."

"So you didn't actually go to bed at midnight. You just took a nap at midnight before going out. Actually, that's very cool. You've been redeemed. I'm gonna buy you a drink."

She left the bar a little later, just as Matt headed in. I told him about my dream and said, "It seemed so real."

"Hmm, no electricity. What did the buildings look like?"

"What do you mean?"

"Did they look the same as they do now—or were they completely different, a different type of architecture?"

"Oh they looked the same as now; they just didn't house the current businesses. Why?"

"Because that narrows it down. If it were some type of past-life dream, or time travel, or astral projection—or a whole myriad of possibilities, the time you were in would probably have been sometime in the 1800's."

I smiled and asked, "Is that your psychic take on it?"

"Oh no. It's actually based entirely on fact. At the end of the 1700's, there were two great fires that destroyed much of the French Quarter. Prior to that, the architecture was different."

"Matt! How do you know all this? No offense, but you don't really strike me as a history buff."

He grinned. "No offense taken. I actually had a job as a tour guide—very briefly."

"I bet that was interesting. Did you like it?"

"It sucked. The tours were at a set time every week, so me showing up whenever I felt like it didn't go over very well."

I laughed and said, "I wouldn't think so."

At work the next night, Erica told me, "I saw you on a horse and buggy yesterday. At least I think I did. Was that you?"

"Yes, it was me, as a matter of fact. That's the first time I ever went on one. It was free too."

"How'd you swing that?"

"Friend of a friend. Well, actually, brother of my boyfriend's friend. My friend now too, I guess."

"Good friend to have."

"Yeah, he's really interesting. He gave us sort of a historical tour along the way."

"Oh cool. I almost called your name when I saw you going by."

"You should have. You could have gotten in on it too."

"Well I didn't know that other guy you and Michael were with."

"Herman. He's in Michael's band. The buggy driver is his brother. Where were you when you saw us?"

"Right by my apartment."

"Oh, we were almost at the end of the line then anyway. He dropped us off on our street."

"Well your day off was a lot more exciting than mine. I just did laundry."

"Was Tony working?"

"No. I haven't seen him in a while."

"Me neither. Dang."

"I know. It's not the same without him."

A bunch of customers started coming in at that point, so we dispersed and started making money. A well-dressed couple at one of my tables asked me what other touristy places they should visit while they were in the Quarter. I suggested, the French Market, Jackson Square, and of course a horse and buggy ride with Quincy.

When I got home that night, Michael said, "Herman gave me the number of that karate instructor."

"Oh good. We're probably a little low on funds for it now, but tape it on the refrigerator, and we'll call one of these days."

"Where's the tape?"

"Just stick it on top of the refrigerator."

"Under the moldy bread?"

"Sure. Hey, I gave out Quincy's business card tonight to a well-dressed couple who seemed interested."

"Oh cool. It's good when people in the Quarter can promote each other."

"And Quincy gives a good tour too. It's funny: I was never really into history before, but for some reason, the history of this place fascinates me."

"Well these few streets have seen so many different things."

"Maybe that's it. This place is more of a character than a location. Still, I don't know. It seems that there's something more, something I can't quite put my finger on. Like a word on the tip of my tongue that I just can't quite remember . . . ."

13

Out with the Girls

The next night, I asked Erica what she was doing after work. Michael already had plans, and I was in the mood for a little escapism and female companionship.

"Thinking about going to Nugent's. Why? What are you in the mood for?"

"Nugent's sounds okay to me."

"See if Katie wants to come too."

Katie did, so we decided to make it a "Girl's Night Out." First we went to Nugent's, and then to Deja Vu. I actually used to hang out at those places more when I first moved there, but even then, usually only with them and after work.

Katie commented, "It's funny how if we don't make plans to go out together, we don't run into each other too much outside of work because we usually hang out at different bars."

It was true too. For professional drinkers like us, you might think any establishment that served liquor would suffice; however, we each seemed to have our own preferences, different places that best suited us according to our personalities. Ambiance was somewhat of a factor, although it didn't necessarily have to be clean or hip. It just has to be comfortable or appealing for whatever reason.

The bartender had a lot to do with it too. And it wasn't just an issue of how generous they were when they poured because, in truth, they were all generous enough. It had more to do with whether or not our personalities clicked.

I said, "Well, I think y'all are a little more uptown, or closer to downtown. I'm a little more outskirts or fringe or whatever. Anyway, let's hit your hangouts; then we can slum over to mine."

Katie smiled. "All right, then Maxwell's is next."

That turned out to be a good choice. It was their Tenth or Thirtieth Anniversary Party; who knows, who cares? Someone bought us all vodka and we got free champagne. We had a social sip to toast the soiree: "May all your loves be true loves, and all your pains be champagnes!"

I said, "Speaking of love, how are your men behaving?"

Katie rolled her eyes. "Oh Danny thought we should have a little space. Wanted to hang out with the guys in his band tonight. Like they don't see enough of each other."

Erica said, "Well at least *you* get a break."

"Yeah, and what about you? How's Jake?"

"Oh, I think the honeymoon's probably over. We've kind of reached that point where we've realized that we don't really have that much in common, but neither one of us wants to give it up yet. There's a certain security in having a comfortable, monogamous relationship."

I sighed. "Oh really? I wouldn't know."

Danny came in at that point, ready for Katie—and looking pleased that he had located her. We saw him swaggering in the door. Katie started fooling with her hair.

I asked, "Up with the hair now?"

She smiled. "Danny likes it up."

He came over, kissed the back of her neck, and they headed out.

Erica and I caught a cab over to Josephine's because we didn't feel like walking. Josie wasn't working, and we didn't know anyone there, but we got a drink and hung out for a little while.

Erica told me, "I caught your comment earlier about the monogamous relationship. So, do you really think he's cheating on you?"

"Hard to tell without any actual proof. And we still have that mad-passion thing going on—sometimes he even acts insanely infatuated with me. I just get the feeling that I'm not the only one he acts that way with."

"Oh, like he's such a superstar."

"Well, he does have a bit of that center stage, inflexible, 'take me as I am,' god mentality, which can make him either irresistible—or downright impossible."

"So where's he playing now?"

He's started his own band, and they're doing some of their own originals. Not those pretty love songs that seduced me when I first met him, he's now doing mostly hard rock. Maybe even metal. What is metal anyway?"

"I don't know—but I'm sure I don't like it."

"Yeah, me neither. Obviously, there's no place for that type of music in the Cover-Tune Quarter, but he found a few clubs uptown that will let him play, although often not for pay. Sometimes the club lets him charge a cover at the door; however, he never brings in much money after he pays the bar tab, then divides the rest—if there's any left— among the band. He and his band members certainly aren't making enough money to live off of. They don't mind though, what do they need money for? They're all living off their girlfriends, who are working double shifts, while they play and flirt with the few groupies that follow them around."

Erica told the bartender to bring us another round and said, "Not that they'd do much better playing cover tunes in the Quarter. Other than a few exceptions, musicians don't typically make a lot of money." She laughed and added, "Or at least they don't end up with a lot."

"That reminds me of that Howlin' Wolf song that says, 'If I had kept all the money that I'd already spent, I would've been a millionaire a long time ago.'"

"Exactly."

"Still, I don't think their music is what New Orleans locals are looking for, although they're getting some flattering write-ups in the paper and have started developing a little following. Occasionally, they also get some tourist who thinks they're hot and wants to get on their mailing list. That's what Michael and I have been fighting about lately. He gave *our* address out to some tourist girls, and they're sending him love letters, which he calls fan mail."

"Give me a break! He's got to be kidding!"

"No. Not kidding. I'm not blind or entirely naïve. I know he flirts with females when he's on the stage, and I can live with that. But I don't know. I just get the feeling that there's more to it than that. There have been little clues, but he denies them all."

"Oh Samantha! You deserve so much better than that. And if Jake ever tries to pull that kind of crap on me, you better tell me the same thing."

"You know I will."

We visited a little longer; then she left, and I headed over to Molly's. They were having a crawfish boil to celebrate something. I don't remember what—an anniversary or birthday or some other excuse to drink too much and party 'til dawn. I passed on the crawfish, but I did have some corn on the cob and a potato that had been boiled right in with the spice. It was delicious.

As the sun started coming up, the bartender sprayed us all over with whipped cream, then got the hose out and hosed us down. I was drenched, but we were all laughing and squealing, of course. Normal people with normal lives probably never saw anything like that—a whipped cream and hose assault at sunrise.

At that point, I went home and Michael still wasn't there. Screw him! Oh well, maybe somebody was. Anyway, he stumbled in about an hour after I got there and passed out beside me. When I awoke from the dead around 5 P.M., he had already left for his gig.

I was off work, but out of food and beverage, so I got dressed and headed out to make groceries. The first time I ever heard somebody say that—*make groceries*, I didn't know what they were talking about, but then I found out that a lot of Louisiana people say that. It comes from the Cajun French translation: *faire des groceries*.

I thought about just stopping at the deli to get a few things, but then I decided to go to the real deal: the A&P. The one in the French Quarter is a narrow-aisled microscopic version of a regular grocery store.

Some guy started following me on the way over there, talking to me the whole way. He had one ring through his nose and two through his lip, but most remarkable about him was his hair. His natural hair was short, but he had several strands of various people's different-colored hair super-glued to it, like extensions.

He told me he was "The Hair Bandit," and he was interested in, and quite determined, to add a strand of my hair to his collection. I told him no, but he was persistent and wouldn't go away. When we got to A&P, he even carried my groceries through the store. As I was checking out, he asked the cashier, "Uh, could you double bag it, please?"

I guess he won me over with the double-bagging request. A few minutes later, he walked off with a huge uneven clump of my hair super-glued to his head. Oh well, my hair was so long and thick and wavy that no one could even tell I was missing any.

I went home and actually cooked some spaghetti. Sometimes I'm just totally in the mood for it. I guess it's the whole tactile experience of winding it around the fork, then draping it over and into my mouth. Eating it takes my mind off everything else because it requires so much attention.

I had just finished when the phone rang. It was some girl calling for Michael. I said, "He's not in; may I ask who's calling?"

She said, "I'll just try back another time," and hung up.

I sat down, put my head in my hands for a minute, thinking *I can't believe this.* Then, I thought, *No, I'm not going to do this. I'm not going to care. There has got to be more to life than this.* Besides, Michael would have some good excuse for it, as he always did: an admiring fan calling to find out when his next gig was . . . .

I headed out and went over to a used bookstore. That always cheered me up. And if not, well, at least it was a melancholy activity that suited me at such times.

On the floor of one of the aisles, there was a man lying down with his head propped up on a stack of books, holding an empty old-fashioned coke bottle in one hand. He was giving a lecture to someone imaginary, or maybe to someone invisible—on how at the center of all things is God.

A woman walked down that aisle and started rummaging through some books. Still sprawled on the floor, the man confidently asked her, "Is there a particular book I can help you find?"

"I'm just looking."

"What topic are you interested in? History? Ah . . . yes, that's a very interesting category."

About ten minutes later, I walked by his aisle and he was still there. He said, "There's that funny girl," giggled, then said, "I mean, that girl again."

I quickly turned down another aisle and he said, "Don't go back there! I wouldn't go back there if I were you. Don't go back there!"

I decided to take his word for it and cleared out of there.

In addition to her job at The Blue, Dana had just started working at Deja Vu part-time, so I went over there to see her. We had sort of become friends. Not forever friends, but *for now* friends. I ordered a drink, then told her about the man at the bookstore.

She asked, "Did he have a long black beard?"

"Yes."

She smiled. "That's my friend."

"You know him?"

"Yeah, he's been around a while. He's schizophrenic, and he lapses in and out of the real world. Sometimes he

acts completely normal. But when he's *out there* . . . well . . .
I know some of it is complete gibberish, but some of it
makes me wonder if he's not tapping into some higher
plane."

"Like what?"

"Oh one time I heard him philosophizing on how
we're all just manifesting as part of the *All*. I don't know. I
don't remember all of it, but it made sense when he
explained it."

"That sounds like something Seth would say."

"Well, some people might think Seth's crazy too." She
smiled and added, "But I like him."

"Me too."

Her shift was almost over, so I hung out with her until
the next bartender arrived, then we headed outside.

Suddenly, a car pulled over, right next to us. A man
leaned out and authoritatively told Dana, "You get in the
back with my friend. Your friend can get in front with me."

Without hesitation, she barked at him, "We're here to
catch a cab, not to pick up Fat Old Men!"

She was always quick with the comebacks. She was
gorgeous and got a lot of attention for that, but she wasn't
sweet, and she wasn't easy. She could out-drink and out-
curse any man, and make him regret it if he didn't treat her
with the respect, dignity, and admiration she deserved.

In some ways, she was my hero, but I didn't want to
be like her. That was her path, not mine.

We waited a few more minutes but there were still no
cabs in sight, so we decided to start walking. Dana asked,
"Did you see all the evangelists out last night?"

"They were hard to miss. When I was walking home,
one of them almost dropped his life-size wooden cross on
me."

"They were screaming at each and every person
walking by, pointing their finger at them, and calling them
a sinner."

"I'm more into love. That fear-based theology just
doesn't do it for me."

"It's definitely a niche group."

We passed The Blue; Seth was just getting off. He walked with us a little bit, and we told him what we had been talking about.

He said, "I believe in God. I just don't necessarily believe in the man-made God that I've found in various churches during my seeking. Personally, I feel God more when I'm helping someone than I ever did going to a particular building at an appointed time every week, especially in churches where the minister was just screaming at everyone."

Dana said, "Amen to that."

I quoted Mark Twain, saying, "In all matters of opinion, our adversaries are insane."

Seth laughed and said, "Well everyone has the freedom to choose whatever works for them. The key is this: whenever something no longer works for you, find something else that does. Keep living. Keep loving."

14

Prison

One unfortunate night soon after that—or early morning, actually, according to the police report, Michael and I went uptown to drink and managed to get ourselves arrested. To this day, neither one of us knows exactly why because we were both in a blackout at the time.

The first thing I do remember is waking up in a jail holding-cell. There were about five other women sitting around. They looked like prostitutes.

I sat up, rubbed my head, looked at the woman next to me, and said, "Oh God, I'm in jail, aren't I?"

"It's not just a bad dream, if that's what you're wondering."

"Did you see me come in?"

"No. You were already passed out here when I came in."

Totally disoriented, I had absolutely no idea what I was doing there. No idea. Couldn't remember anything at that point. I just sat up and looked around, confused.

Then it slowly came back to me, a little of it anyway. I could vaguely remember a moment of crying in the back of the cop car. Michael had been sitting next to me, and we were both handcuffed. He was gallantly pleading with the cops to let me go and just take him. Of course they were ignoring him. I couldn't remember anything after that.

The door opened, and one of the guards looked in and noticed I was awake. I don't know how long I had been sleeping. Sleeping, passed out, unconscious, whatever . . . .

He left, but soon after that, someone came and got me, and he took me and booked me, or whatever it is that they do. I don't remember them taking my picture or anything like that, but the man behind the teller window did take my purse; then he wrote down a list of the contents inside. I had eighteen dollars in there. I asked if he could give me change from my money so I could get a pack of cigarettes and make a phone call. I normally don't smoke, just an occasional drag now and then, but I wanted a pack anyway. I was in the mood.

The guard escorted me to the cigarette machine. Then, as we continued walking down the hall, I asked him, "Hey, what about my one phone call?"

He told me, "Actually you can make as many as you want. There's a phone in the holding cell."

I called Dana. Luckily she answered the phone because I think I would have been mortified to call anyone else. There was no feeling mortified around Dana. You were just either afraid of her—or you weren't. Fortunately, I wasn't. Not anymore anyway. I told her everything I knew, and she said she'd see what she could do.

The holding cell had about twenty women squeezed inside of it. It was apparently lunchtime by then, because someone came by with a tray of sandwiches and started passing them out. I still felt drunk and a little nauseous, so I told the guard, "I don't want one, but you can give mine to her (pointing to another woman) because she's skinny and looks like she could use an extra."

That was obviously a mistake. She started coming at me, spewing, "Who you calling skinny? You're skinny, you skinny little bitch. I'll beat the shit out of you!"

I quickly told her, "I'm so sorry; I really didn't mean it bad! I swear! I just said that so they would give my food to you, rather than throw it away."

"Well, watch who you call skinny next time, Bitch," she said as she grabbed my sandwich and backed away, still keeping an eye on me.

I had only been in jail for a short while, and I had already learned that it would probably be better to keep my mouth shut. I was scared of that woman, but, as it turned out, I didn't have to worry about her for much longer because I wasn't in there for very long.

There was some kind of mix-up or something because when they came to make a pickup to take some ladies to the official New Orleans Prison, they took me! They loaded me up in a van, shackled me in, and drove me over. I kept asking what was going on, but they didn't bother to answer.

When I got there, two female guards had me take off all my clothes and made me bend over and spread so that they could examine every nook and cranny. I told them, "I don't understand why I'm over here. I was drunk, but I wasn't driving or anything."

"Really? There must be some mistake," one of them said, as if she really didn't care. "Oh well, we can't do anything about it. We still have to go through our procedures here," and they continued with the strip search.

After that, I was required to take a shower, while several women sat at a picnic table nearby and watched. I had never taken a shower in front of an audience before. One of the women kept eyeing me up and down and licking her lips. I felt uncomfortable and a little embarrassed and tried to get it over with as quickly as possible.

A guard handed me a towel to dry off with and a prison uniform to wear. A prison uniform!

For a little while, I hung out in a large community room with probably about a hundred other prisoners, watching TV and visiting. I was very popular. A lot of the women came over to talk to me, to find out why I was there, and to get to know me. Most of them wanted a cigarette, so my pack didn't last very long at all. Good thing I wasn't a regular smoker. I was feeling really nervous though, especially after I had handed out my last cigarette and had nothing left to hand out.

Around that time, we were given the option to stay in that big room or be locked in our cell. I chose the cell over staying with the big group. Before leaving me there, the guard gave me a toothbrush, toothpaste, and a bar of soap.

Fortunately, my roommate was very nice. The cell had two beds, a toilet, and a sink. We had a window in there, with bars on it of course. The men were all hanging out in the courtyard below. We were checking them out, and my roommate was looking for her boyfriend, but she didn't see him.

We did see some other cute guys though. We were pointing out different ones, commenting, and laughing. It almost reminded of college when my roommate and I used to check out guys in the courtyard outside our dorm. *Except for then, I wasn't wearing a prison uniform!*

Finally, one of the guards came and got me, handed me my clothes, and told me to get dressed. Dana had gotten a bail-bondsman to get me out.

I walked out, smiled, and said, "I've been sprung!" Then I looked around and asked, "Where's Michael?"

"He was in the regular holding cell the whole time, so they were able to get him out quicker. He actually already caught a cab to work. There was a little more paperwork and confusion in getting you out since they had transferred you to the women's prison."

"Well, that about sums up our relationship: I'm doing *time* while he's just getting ready for his next gig. Anyway, I can't believe they put me over here! Everyone said it was a mistake."

"Everyone who?"

"My fellow inmates. I made a few friends."

She laughed and said, "Of course you did, Samantha. You'll have to tell me all about it. But yeah, it probably was a mistake. They said it was because the holding cells were too crowded at the other place. Do you want to go get something to eat?"

"Please! I've been locked up for fifteen hours and haven't eaten anything."

"Where do you want to go?"

"The first place you see."

We stopped at a fast food place. While we ate, Dana asked, "So, how was prison?"

Sarcastically I answered, "Oh, it was wonderful, really. I had a great time. I never knew how exhilarating showering in front of a bunch of women could be. It was empowering in a Get-me-out-of-here-before-someone-takes-me kind of way."

"You took a shower there?"

"Yes while a bunch of women watched me."

"Oh you poor thing! You're so little and cute they were probably ready to eat you alive."

"I managed to hold them off with cigarettes, for a few minutes anyway, until the pack ran out. Fortunately, we had the option of being locked in our cells around that time."

"So you were actually locked in a cell?"

"Yeah, with my roommate."

"You had a roommate?"

"Yes, she was really nice though. Couldn't have asked for better. Got busted on some drug thing. Nice girl though, really."

"I'm sure she was."

"Did I mention I was wearing a prison uniform?"

"No," she said, looking as if nothing more could surprise her.

"Yes, and they took away my bra and my shoelaces while I was in there too."

"What for?"

"The bra because it had an underwire which could be used as a weapon, and the shoelaces so I wouldn't hang myself."

"They obviously had no idea what you're really like."

"Nor did they care. I realized that right away. They were treating me as if I might be in there for months—or longer. Believe me, there are lots of people in there claiming that they don't really belong there. The guards have heard it all before, and they don't care. I can totally see how someone could get lost in the system."

"Bet you were happy to see me."

"You have no idea how much."

"They give you a court date?"

"Yes, and they said I could have a court-appointed attorney. That should be good enough. It's not like I was driving or anything."

"What exactly were you arrested for?"

"Not sure exactly because I was in a blackout."

"You don't remember anything?"

"Not a thing. But according to the arrest report, it looks like I was drunk in public outside of a twenty-four hour bar. It's a twenty-four hour bar! What do they expect?"

"Which bar was it?"

I gave her the name and she said, "The cops are hell in that district. Next time you oughta get drunk in a different district."

"Or just stick to the Quarter. No one bothers us there."

"Except for the tourists, and we know how to handle them."

She dropped me off at home, and I just stayed in that night, somewhat in a daze. I was off work, so I had time to process the experience.

It did seem unbelievable that I had gone to prison, been strip searched, and had my underwire bra and shoelaces taken from me just for being drunk in public—standing outside a twenty-four hour bar! Was it all just a mistake, or was it some type of cosmic wake-up call?

Certainly I don't think that being a drunk pedestrian merited that type of consequence. However, I had been living on the wild side and might not have been heading down a good road. Nothing like an accidental trip to prison to get me thinking about my lifestyle.

I don't think Michael had any similar type of reflection. He had gotten off easier and earlier, even used a fake name, then went straight on to his gig. Oh well, this wasn't his story or his life. It was mine.

Soon after that, in an effort to make some type of change in our lives, Michael and I decided to start taking karate. I had always wanted to take it: to learn how to defend myself in case I ever needed to, but also as a spiritual discipline.

I called the man Herman had recommended, and signed us up to take classes twice a week. It was a new time slot, and Michael and I were the only ones who had signed up for it, so we'd essentially be getting private lessons without having to pay extra for them.

When we arrived at the dojo, we met our instructor—or sensei. I noticed that he had that same type of present-look in his eyes that Seth had. He gave us white uniforms, and we headed back to the dressing rooms to put them on.

In the back of the dojo, there was an active voodoo altar with several lit candles. I nudged Michael and nodded over to it. He looked, raised his eyebrows and shrugged. We didn't say anything to our instructor about it, and he didn't say anything about it either. Not then anyway. He did tell us that he incorporated Zen and meditation into his lessons, and we began the class with a meditation.

Then he told us a little about his philosophy, saying that some martial art schools just teach people how to fight, and some students just study martial arts to expand and enhance their fighting skills. He said, "That's not my philosophy. For me, it's a spiritual discipline, a moving meditation. I teach martial arts to instill confidence as well as serenity, so that while my students are able to defend themselves when necessary, they are often able to do so without fighting."

His philosophy was more in line with mine than with Michael's. Maybe it was easier for me though, being a woman. On one hand, women are more likely to be raped or mugged than men; however, a man is more likely to attack another man in a bar-fight. Most, although not all, of the violence I've witnessed in my life involved some guys fighting each other in a rage.

As for me, I always chose verbal diplomacy over physical aggression. Not Michael. He got a lot more hands-on practice than I did. For him, our karate class did increase his skills, and he was able to put those new skills into use at a big brawl that took place at Josephine's one night.

He and I were sitting off to the side, warming up by the fireplace. It was rarely lit, but it was really cozy when it was. We suddenly heard voices getting louder, and looked over toward the bar to see what was going on.

Three redneck tourists had started insulting a local drag queen who frequented the bar. Apparently, they didn't realize that the drag queen fit in better there than they did. Josie told the rednecks to leave. They may have been thinking about it, but they didn't immediately act on it, so one of the locals decided to assist them to the door. They didn't take that well, and they started throwing punches at him. Some other local guy ran over to assist; they grabbed pool sticks and started thrashing him with those. A third local jumped in; they put him on the ground.

Then, Superhero Michael jumped in, flew around the bar, and saved the day. He soon had the bad guys on the ground, and he was doing his favorite thing—kicking.

After the rednecks managed to get up, they moved on.

Everyone started rehashing, and some guy with a serious Southern drawl told Michael, "You must know that Tah-kwon-do." We all busted out laughing.

While the guys bonded and warmly discussed the details of the fight, Josie and I had our own conversation.

She said, "Michael saves the day."

I laughed. "Yeah. He's a lover *and* a fighter."

She poured us each a shot of Jagermeister. We drank it, then she told me, "The ironic thing about it is that if the guys hadn't tried to help me, I probably could have gotten the rednecks to leave on my own. Sometimes men are more likely to listen to a woman in that type of situation. I can firmly tell someone to leave and insist upon it, and they do.

But then if a guy jumps in to assist me, the person refuses to leave, and it turns into a fight."

"That's been my experience too. If a guy steps in to help, then it becomes more of an ego issue. Sometimes it would be better if they'd stay out of it."

"Maybe bouncers should be women."

"Well sometimes we do need brutal male strength when a situation is already out of control. But I think it is a good idea to start with feminine diplomacy first and see if that will work before jumping in with the heavy-breathing, huffing-puffing, muscle-flexing, vein-popping type of assistance."

15
Expunged and a Full Moon

Michael didn't have to go to court over the arrest because he had given the cops a fake name and hadn't had any identification on him to prove otherwise.

As for me, I went on my assigned day, dressed as respectably as I could, and met Ethan, my court-appointed attorney.

He told me, "I know this sounds like a line, but you look really familiar to me. I don't know where I would have seen you before though."

He actually looked a little familiar to me too, but I didn't tell him that. I just looked into his pretty blue eyes, smiled, and shrugged.

My case actually ended up getting dismissed anyway because the cop who had arrested us didn't even show up. Afterward, Ethan gave me his business card, and said, "Call me if you have any questions, or if you ever need anything, or if you just want to talk."

I didn't, but not long after that, he called me and said, "I'm calling for two reasons. First of all, I thought you were really sweet, and I wanted to see if you'd like to go out with me sometime."

Feeling bad, I said, "I'm sorry—I can't because I have a boyfriend."

"That's all right. I figured you probably did, but I'd still like to help you out. That's the second reason I called. I can get your case expunged, and it won't cost you anything."

"Expunged? What does that mean? Wasn't my case already dismissed?"

"Yes, but the arrest and the hearing are all still on record. For minor cases like this, it is possible to get it expunged, so that, essentially, it will be completely erased, and no one will ever be able to pull this information up about you."

"That sounds good. What do I have to do?"

"Just sign a paper, and I'll take care of the rest. I can bring it by your place, or I can meet you somewhere. Anywhere you want."

I chose Café du Monde because it was easy to get to, and I figured he'd know where it was. He did, of course. I skimmed over the papers. It all looked legitimate, so I went ahead and signed it.

He told me, "Since this is probably as close to a date with you as I'm going to get, at least let me pay for your coffee."

"Okay, thanks. And I really appreciate you doing this for me."

"No problem. If you ever need anything or if you ever break up with your boyfriend and want to go out sometime, give me a call."

"Thanks, Ethan. You're a really nice guy. It's good to know that there are guys like you out there."

He smiled. "How do you know I'm a nice guy?"

"Because you offered me the expunged deal even after I turned you down."

He took a sip of his coffee and just looked at me for a moment, then said, "I don't even know why I did it. I've never done this before."

"Never done what before?"

"Called up a client like this after a case. I actually felt nervous too. It took me days to finally go through with making the phone call. So, when you said you couldn't go out with me because you had a boyfriend, I had really already anticipated that. But there's just something about you. I don't know what it is. When I first saw you, I really did feel as if I already knew you."

I went back home and told Michael all about it—he didn't mind. He never got overtly jealous. He wanted me to be his main and primary lover, but maybe not his only . . . .

He had talked to me about that early in our relationship, and I had told him that I needed a sexually monogamous relationship—dictated by sanity, common sense, and the will to live, and that if he needed that type of open relationship, that he should just let me go and move on. He had thought about it, decided that he couldn't live without me, and from that point forward, he tried, I guess. I really think he tried.

He was a lover; he had a lot of love; he wanted to spread his love around. We went out that night and ended up getting into a dramatic and impassioned fight about it.

I had to go to work the next night. When I walked in, Jennifer took one look at me and asked, "You ready for a drink?"

"I don't know. I feel kind of weird."

"Well Samantha, you are kind of weird."

I said, "Thank you," knowing that she meant it as a compliment, went ahead and got my drink, then told her, "I've got this bruise on my head from banging it against the wall . . . or maybe I got it when I took that nasty fall. You know this past week's really been a mess."

She laughed. "Tell me about it! I got way too messed up last night—even for me—and did something really stupid. I still can't believe it."

Intuitively I said, "You slept with the sax player."

"Yes! How'd you know?"

"That y'all secretly have a thing for each other? Please! Everyone knows."

"Oh my God. I feel terrible. I can't even look over to the stage to see if he's here yet."

"He's not. What happened?"

"I don't even want to talk about it. I'm so embarrassed."

"Was last night a full moon or something? Because I was a bad girl too. I got rip-roaring drunk, picked a fight with Michael, and walked to The Abbey all by myself."

"Samantha! Well, now I don't feel so bad."

"Yeah, whenever Michael and I don't hook up or we're fighting or something, I can just walk over to The Abbey— or run if it's a dark and lonely night—and it's open twenty-four hours, seven days a week, waiting for me almost."

"So what led up to it?"

"I don't remember word-for-word, except to say that it was our usual . . . about some other woman. I do remember my last words to him though as I left Josephine's. I told him, 'We are through, t-h-r-o-u-g-h, through!' And he didn't follow me, so I just headed over to The Abbey.

"That was dramatic."

"He says that I always have to have the last word. Well, sure, if I think I can pull it off."

"Of course, why not? So what happened after that?"

"I'm not sure exactly. The last thing I remember is standing on a stool, singing Louis Armstrong's 'What a Wonderful World' at the top of my lungs, along with the jukebox. I don't actually sing it; I do some kind of throaty accompaniment. Wonder how I got home."

Jennifer laughed. "Now I really don't feel so bad."

"Yeah, today Michael and I were rehashing last night's argument. You know, recapping on the highlights, and I didn't think it would be a good time to ask him how I got home."

"You don't remember anything after 'What a Wonderful World'?"

"No. Nothing. He might've come and got me though. He's done that before: comes looking for me, then he'll just throw me over his shoulder and carry me all the way home. It's not fair really because when I go looking for him, I never find him. But if I'm not home by 6 A.M., then I'm probably at The Abbey, which for some reason, I think of as my hiding place. Who knew I'd turn out to be so predictable?"

"Samantha! You've made me feel so much better. Last night I just freaked. You know what he said to me? 'I'll still respect you in the morning.' I just freaked all the sudden, like I didn't know what I was doing there, said, 'I gotta go,' and left. I can't even look at the stage."

"Well he's here now, and you'd better talk to him on the break. At least say, 'Hi,' because the longer you avoid him, the more awkward it's going to be."

"You're right," she said, as she glanced over at the stage nervously. "I should, but that doesn't mean I will."

Erica was off that night; another girl was working. She told us that she and her boyfriend had also had a big fight the night before, in some little bar where they were partying: "Whenever I drink Tequila, I always start turning into an exhibitionist. I just can't help it."

She had pulled her skirt up and flashed her boyfriend and his friend. Initially he had egged her on a couple of times with his, "Ooh Baby, Baby," but then he got pissed off when she started liking it a little too much and got carried away. He bitched her out and made her feel stupid. She cried and told him she never wanted to see him again.

I summed it up for all of us: "Alcohol makes strangers love, and lovers fight."

Jennifer added, "You got that right."

I made it through the rest of my shift, then went straight home. Michael wasn't there yet. I fell asleep and had a bizarre dream about Ethan, but I couldn't remember the details of it when I woke up.

16

Hungover Angst

The next night, Michael and I—fully reconciled, for the time being anyway—got drunk and went to Tipitina's. This time, however, as far as I know, we did not go backstage. We did not party with the band afterward. As a matter of fact, I don't even remember leaving Tipitina's, although I do vaguely remember something about someone hitting a streetcar with their car, but I don't know if it involved the car we were riding in, or if someone told me about it, or if it was a dream I had.

Oh well, someone may have had a wreck, and it may have been us. Not actually us—we didn't have a car. But perhaps some acquaintance or stranger we had caught a ride with. The next day, I was trying to remember, but Michael was no help. He didn't know. He didn't remember any of it.

I had a splitting headache from drinking too much—it certainly wasn't the first time either. Maybe it had something to do with working on Bourbon Street and living in the French Quarter. I lay there, feeling like a bloated cotton ball, thought about it for a while, and concluded that I'd probably drink nearly every day until I was out of the rut; therefore, I needed to start taking steps to try to get out.

At work, other than Seth, the bartenders, waitresses, and band members drank every shift that they worked—not an occasional wine spritzer here or there, I'm talking shots with vodka chasers. Serious drinkers—you couldn't even tell they'd been drinking until their shift was over and then they'd either go to another bar where they'd continue drinking, or they'd go home and pass out.

The managers really did look the other way. Anyway, they were off into their various forms of escapism. Roger had once told me that the only reason any of us were in this business is that we lack discipline . . . so possibly true.

Most of the people I knew drank, some of them drank and did drugs, some of them didn't drink, but they did drugs. I didn't really know anyone who abstained from everything.

Drugs that I had personally witnessed people using were marijuana, cocaine, ecstasy, LSD, valium, xanax, as well as various muscle relaxants. Marijuana (weed, herb, ganja) was so widely and frequently used as to not even be considered illegal—except maybe by some of the cops. Waitresses and bartenders smoked it in the bathroom; band members, managers, and club owner's smoked it in the office. Other people smoked it around corners, in parking lots, or even just walking down the street.

Not me. I had discovered that I actually preferred to just drink. I didn't want anything to interfere with the consistent alcohol buzz that I liked to maintain.

My relationship with Michael had survived all the intricacies of the Quarter, had survived a lot of things, but now we were fighting, often talking about breaking up, yet never actually going through with it.

At the beginning, we had agreed on everything, which sounds unrealistic, I know. There just wasn't one single thing that seemed important enough to disagree about. Lately, it seemed we'd disagree on everything. I'd say, "I'm cold," and he'd immediately say, "It's not cold." Or I'd say, "It's cloudy," and he'd pipe in with, "It's not that cloudy."

Yes, we'd disagree on everything, except for when we were drinking. Fortunately, we were usually drinking.

I found him easier to tolerate when I had a little alcohol in me. Actually, I had even started sneaking drinks around him sometimes. I don't know why. If we were both home in the afternoon, sometimes I'd go to the kitchen and act like I was getting water, but really I'd get a vodka and water. I could have told him about it, or asked him if he wanted a drink or whatever, but I didn't. I liked hanging out in our apartment and having a drink without him knowing—like I had a secret too.

Ogden Nash said that he drank to make other people more interesting. I drank to make them less irritating.

The disagreements had started with the trust issue, or lack thereof. They started around the same time the fan stuff started coming to our apartment. It just didn't all seem fan-related.

Another thing is that at the beginning of our relationship we always did laundry together: first at the laundromat on the corner, then at CheckPoint Charlie's. We always made it fun too.

Well, Michael rarely even did laundry anymore, so I had started going to the laundromat on the corner again, and most of the time I did his laundry too. But he wasn't there and Tony wasn't there anymore either, and it wasn't fun anymore; now it was just a stupid, lonely chore. Maybe that's all it is for most people, just a stupid, necessary chore. But it really had been a fun event for us for a while. Now it was a non-event, a drudgery, a bore.

I had been working at The Blue almost all that time. I was barely paying my bills each month and hadn't saved a dime. Didn't want to live with Michael anymore. Was definitely time for a change!

Bianca called while I was deep in the midst of my hung-over angst. She told me, "Your parents called, well your mom did. She wanted me to try to talk you into going back to school."

I snorted and said, "Well that proposal couldn't have come at a worse time. Things are really going great for me here now. Last week, it may have been tempting, but today I'm going to have to pass."

"She wanted to know how you're doing, Sam. Wanted to make sure you're okay. She just wants what's best for you."

"No, actually both my parents want what they think is best for me. Although I guess that's the way all parents are."

"That's cool, Sam. I just wanted to let you know. You know I'm on your side. I'm always on your side."

"That's because you're part of my true family."

"That's right, sister."

I hung up and considered calling my mother for a minute, even wanted to for a millisecond maybe, then hesitated and thought, "To hell with it!"

Franz Kafka had said, "Between being lost and being found, there is the unconsciousness of being lost: the only true agony, as when a foot that was asleep begins to wake up."

Things might not seem so great right now, but this was just a temporary downtime, a chaotic lull in an otherwise fascinating life. I started singing Frank Sinatra's "New York, New York" and belted out, "I pick myself up and get back in the race!" as I got dressed and headed out.

Things would turn around, right? I knew I was drinking too much, but I knew I could stop if wanted to. I just didn't want to yet, not while I was still living and working in the Quarter . . . definitely not today anyway.

17

I Hate Myself for Loving You

Michael had already left for his gig earlier. I had been scheduled to work, but at the last minute, I called and got somebody from the early shift to work for me. Then I headed over to the club where Michael was playing.

When I walked in, he looked over at me from the stage, smiled, and said, "Hello Sweetheart," into the microphone. He was in the middle of a song, but he just blended it in.

The waitress was serving a drink to a red-haired woman sitting by herself at a front table. After the woman paid for the drink, she turned around and saw me standing there. She got up and left the club, never even taking a sip of the drink she had just ordered and paid for.

After the gig, I asked Michael about it, asked who she was. He denied knowing her or even noticing that it had occurred, but I knew that was a lie because he always noticed everything.

He told me, "You were the most beautiful woman in the club tonight, in all of New Orleans maybe, and besides, you're Samantha—my Sammi, so you don't have anything to worry about. And you're the only woman I'm going home to tonight, the only woman I want to go home to."

I knew he was laying it on thick, but I let him console me, let him be my consolation prize . . . at least for the night.

The next day, the doorbell rang. Michael and I raced each other to look out the window. We didn't see anyone, but there was a UPS truck down there. Michael went downstairs to check it out, then came back up carrying a big box addressed to him.

It was full of clothes—sent by one of his groupie girls. They weren't even cool clothes either. They were a little too cowboy for our scene. But still, it made me sick that someone else had gone shopping for him.

Naturally I got upset and tried to talk to him about it. He ran his fingers through my hair and told me, "Don't worry about it. It's no big deal. You don't have anything to be jealous about."

"I'm not jealous. I just don't see why somebody is sending you clothes."

"Seriously Sammi, this is nothing. Some tourist asked for my address when she was in town, said she wanted to send me something from Switzerland. I thought she'd send us some good chocolates."

"Well maybe this one is no big deal, but what about the phone calls? Some girl has been calling and hanging up when I answer? Or sometimes she gives me a message for you—as if I were your sister or something."

He put both his arms around me and said, "Oh, you're definitely not my sister, darling."

"I just don't feel that I can trust you."

He stepped back and said, "Look, I can't give up on my dreams and goals and throw my whole life away just because you're feeling jealous. I try to make you realize that you're the most important woman to me, but it doesn't seem to be enough."

"I've never asked you to give up your dreams and goals. I've supported you on that."

"Well, I'm a musician. Women look at me. That's not going to change. But I've found the woman I love, and I'd marry you tomorrow if you were willing. You're the one who doesn't want to."

"I don't like feeling this way . . . worrying about if I can trust you or not. I just can't make that go away."

He looked angry, said, "If that's really how you feel, maybe I should just leave." Then he headed for the door.

I got there first, stood in front of the door handle, and said, "Michael, please don't leave. Stay and lets talk about this."

He started to say something, then stopped. His face got softer, and he told me, "Look, I know it feels as if you can't trust me—can't trust anybody maybe—I feel that way sometimes too. But that's why we have to trust each other—we need each other. You have to believe in something, Sammi. Believe in us."

I was already feeling very fragile, and that pushed me over the edge. I sank to the floor in tears.

He eased down beside me and gently said, "It's okay, Sammi. It's okay." He wrapped his arms around me and kissed away my tears, saying, "I know I'm not perfect. I screw up a lot. But I love and accept you for who you are. Can't you just accept me as I am? Please?" He actually started crying while he said it, with tears running down his cheeks to match my own. How could that not move me? He seemed very sincere . . . and I loved him deeply.

Still, although part of me wanted to believe him, part of me couldn't. I tried to go to all of his gigs, not because I was a fan of the music, but rather because I didn't trust him if I wasn't there. I know that sounds terrible too. I wrestled with that fact: that if I had that little trust in him, I should have gone ahead and split up with him then, but I just wasn't ready to give it up yet.

Soon after that, I wasn't able to go to one of his gigs because I couldn't get off work. When I got home after my shift, he still wasn't there and didn't even bother to come home that night at all, didn't show up until noon the next day.

That night, I actually made it over to Josephine's before midnight. I wasn't sure if it was Josie's night off or not. Seeing her standing behind the bar was the highlight of an otherwise miserably pathetic day.

She looked up surprised and said, "I thought you were working tonight."

"I was supposed to, but I got some new girl to work for me. I just couldn't handle it tonight. I've already got the blues."

"What did he do this time?" she asked as she handed me a drink.

"He didn't come home last night, didn't even call. When he finally showed up at noon today, he had some totally lame excuse about partying with some male acquaintance of his and passing out at the guy's apartment. I told him that it was a bunch of crap, and that there was no reason he couldn't have called me, and that I wanted him to pack his shit and move out."

"Oh my God! Are you serious?"

"Well, all of it except for the part about me telling him to pack his shit and move out."

"Samantha!"

"Well that's what I should have said though. I wish I would have said it. Instead we had some pathetic little fight and then made up. I hate myself for being so weak. That's not the me that I want to be."

She said, "Hold on! I've got a song for you," went over to the jukebox, and put Joan Jett's song on "I Hate Myself for Loving You." We both sang it at the top of our lungs with our long hair flying everywhere, hers in braids of course. It cheered me up immensely.

After that, she asked, "Is there anything else I can do to help?"

I smiled. "Braid my hair."

"Braid your hair?"

"Yes. Just like yours."

She came and sat on the stool next to me and started braiding.

A man came in with his parrot and camera. I had seen him over in Jackson Square sometimes taking pictures of tourists with his bird. Josie started to stand up to ask him what he wanted to drink. He told her, "No, that's okay. I'll wait."

When she finished, he took a picture of Josie and me standing next to each other with our matching braids. She hung it up on the wall behind the bar. We did look pretty cute.

Thank God for Josie. She helped me keep my sanity and some sense of self—and even have a sense of humor about it sometimes—when all I really felt like doing was crawling into a hole somewhere.

18

Incognito on Halloween

Two days before Halloween, some man ordered a drink and gave me a fifty-dollar tip. Since it seemed like extra money, I decided to splurge on a Halloween costume. I got a strange mask that made me look like a wise old man, and a long white robe.

The coolest thing about the outfit was that no one could tell who I was, or even whether I was a man or a woman. It was a unique opportunity to walk through the French Quarter streets incognito, something I was never able to do anymore since everyone from the street thugs to the antique store owners at least knew my face by then. Michael by my side would have been a dead give-a-way as to my identity, but since we were temporarily fighting, I was flying solo for the evening.

I decided to start at the back of the Quarter and work my way forward. First I went to CheckPoint Charlie's where a cool band was playing, and there were actually a couple of people doing laundry in costume. The "Cocktails? Cigarettes? French fries?" bartender was dressed up like a French maid. He was even more entertaining and lively than usual.

Next, I went by The Abbey where I ran into some guy who we called "Slick." He always flirted with everybody, but he was harmless.

I pulled my mask off so that he could see who I was and asked him, "What are you supposed to be?"

He told me, "I am still the Master Bum. Can I ask you a question? Do you still love me?"

I smiled and said, "*Still* would imply that I did at one time. But believe whatever you want to, darling, if it gets you through the night."

He laughed and asked, "Have you seen Luna anytime recently?" referring to his ex-girlfriend.

"No, not since the last time I saw you both at Molly's. Are y'all back together?"

"No, but I still care about her. Anyway, do you know her last name?"

"No, I don't even know your last name. Why?"

"She got arrested last Friday, and no one's seen her since. We can't find out any information about her because no one knows her last name. Luna might not even be her real first name. Anyway, she might just be sitting in jail."

"Well, good luck. Just keep asking around. Someone might know."

"Can you believe I lived with her for six months, maybe longer, and I don't even know her last name?"

"Actually, that is a little hard to believe . . . ."

That's how it was with last names though. Most of the people in the French Quarter that I associated with didn't know my last name. No one even asked. The only time it came up was on employment or apartment applications.

Michael's driver's license had been revoked at some point, and he never replaced it with any form of identification. He played gigs where he always got paid in cash, and he wasn't officially on my lease. If it weren't for the fact that I actually met his parents one time, he could have even been lying to me about his name.

If you needed to work under the table and live off the radar, the French Quarter was still a place you could do that.

It wasn't the *"What's your name? Who's your daddy? Is he rich like me?"* kind of town, like the one I had grown up in. It was more of a *"Don't care who you are; you look interesting. Do you wanna spend some time with me?"* kind of place.

As a community, it may have appeared more intimate than it was. We were all on a first name basis; however, that's about all we knew about each other. Well, to be fair, we may have known each other's dreams, but not each other's backgrounds, and, in the long-term picture, we wouldn't necessarily share each other's lives. Some did though. Some people chose to live there forever.

I left The Abbey and headed over to The Blue, still in full costume. Roger led me to a table, and I sat down. Erica came over and took my order. Neither one of them, nor anyone else there for that matter, had any idea who I was. I took my mask off and showed Erica when she brought my drink, and she told Roger, and so on, and everybody thought it was really funny, and of course, Roger wouldn't let me pay for my drink.

Erica went off to serve some other customers, then came back and told me that she and Jake had actually had their first fight. "Over nothing, really. I think I was just looking for an excuse."

"An excuse for what?"

"For him to stop boring me maybe? I don't know. We're just very different, and I get the feeling he has absolutely no interest in finding out more about me. It's always all about him."

"Well he's definitely missing out."

"Thanks Samantha! If only you'd have been there last night telling me that. But no, I just made up with him so everything could be nice between us again. But his time's almost up."

I left there and went to Josephine's, where Michael finally caught up with me. By then, I wasn't mad at him anymore and, in fact, could barely even remember what it was we had been fighting about. He wasn't concerned about it anymore either. Not that any of the underlying issues had been resolved, we just both chose temporary amnesia.

Not wanting to come out without a costume, he had pulled our purple velvet curtain off the window and wrapped it around himself like a cape. I didn't know what he was exactly, but then again I didn't know what I was exactly either, and at that point, it didn't even matter.

19

French Quarter Characters

A normal night for us at work generally had at least one weird, violent, or perverted act, but some nights were so exaggerated that they went beyond weird. This was one of them.

Fortunately, Roger had another manager working with him that night to help with crowd control. Jimmy was a lot more upbeat and happy-go-lucky than Roger, but they worked well together.

Roger? Not so happy-go-lucky. He had one of those bodies that looked as if he had started lifting weights at too young of an age. He would lumber over to potential customers, chest puffing out, and ask them if they wanted a table as if he were challenging them with, "What did you say about my mother!" Then, as he went to seat them, he would do a little move where it looked like he was trying to get his underwear out of his butt without using his hands. I think that was part of his tough guy walk. And it wasn't just an act either. He was prepared to follow through on it—and often did.

That night he did. One guy started a fistfight with a guy at the table next to him. My macho managers took the problem into their own hands: Roger pulled and Jimmy pushed. When they got to the doorway, they literally threw him out—his feet did leave the ground—headfirst onto the pavement.

The guy sat there rubbing his head for a minute, with a bewildered, "Why'd you do that to me?" look on his face. Then he stood up unsteadily and approached the doorway. Roger and Jimmy's chests immediately puffed out like blow-up dolls, and they started breathing heavily, as if they had learned it in Lamaze class. They pointed down the road, and fortunately for the guy, he took their advice.

As they victoriously paraded back into the bar, Dana shouted out, "Teamwork!" and they broke into huge proud smiles. For about an hour after that, they kept looking at each other with a glow and a secret grin, as if they had just had sex together or something.

Erica said, "I wonder when Roger slammed that guy's head . . . if he really did any damage."

I told her, "I've wondered the same thing myself because I've seen him bust plenty of people's heads open."

"Really? Busted open?"

"Well I didn't see their brains or anything. But blood gushing . . . yeah, I've seen lots of that." I said it matter-of-factly too, as if it didn't really phase me much anymore. It's strange how your comfort zone, your threshold, the line you won't cross, can slowly get pushed out further and further.

Fights would often bring up fond memories of other brawls and conquests for Roger. He came over and told me with a cocky smile, "I bit part of a guy's ear off once, got him right in the jugular."

"Oh yeah? What was that for?"

He puffed his chest out some more and said, "We were having a little difference of opinion on who was going to live and who wasn't."

About an hour later, Roger rushed over from the door and said, "Call the cops! There's a fight right outside the bar!"

I relayed the message, then neglected my customers to run outside and see what was going on.

Two guys were going at it. Neither one of them could've weighed over a hundred and forty pounds. They appeared to be drunk. The guy in green knocked the guy clutching his hat to the ground, then lost his own balance, fell, and slammed his own head into the brick wall. He recovered, crawled over to the guy he had just landed, and got some more punches in. He stood up, gave the guy a final kick, and screamed, "Get up! Get up!"

When the guy did get up, he ran across the street. The guy in green walked off the other way; then suddenly, he ran back toward the other guy, and they went at it again. The guy in green dominated again, knocked the other guy down, and then stomped on him until he was unconscious.

The cops finally showed up. First attempts to revive the guy proved unsuccessful. It took about ten minutes for them to bring him around. The cops tried to stand him up a couple of times, and each time he crumpled to the ground. Well I wasn't surprised; his legs had been stomped on several times. Finally, they got him up, but he was walking unsteadily, falling down and getting back up again.

They handcuffed the guy in green and took him off to jail. The other guy tried to walk off, fell again, and they took him off in an Emergency Care Unit to the Hospital. All the while, he was still clutching his crumpled hat, being careful to replace it back on his head every time it fell off.

After witnessing that, I felt like throwing up, but drank a shot of Midori, Bailey's and Vodka instead.

At the end of the night, I thought Michael might be waiting for me outside. I don't know why. The night had been upsetting; maybe I was just hoping he would be.

Things had been kind of weird between us though. We'd been fighting more often than not, but for some reason I still wanted us to act normal toward each other, to still play out the boyfriend/girlfriend act.

I guess he wasn't comfortable pretending or acting as if we were getting along because he didn't show up, so I headed over to Nugent's with a couple of people and had a drink or two. It felt empty, but at least it was something. I didn't want to go straight home to the possibility of him not being there, not that night.

When I got home a little while later, he was there, but he was already asleep. I wanted to curl up next to him, maybe even wake him, but I didn't. Couldn't handle the rejection if he were to turn over and roll away from me. Instead, I just got as close to him as I could without actually disturbing him.

He had sort of shut me out lately, and that was hurting me more than the suspected infidelity. If he had been unfaithful, maybe he was feeling guilty about it and that was why he was shutting me out. But I hated being shut out more than anything! That crushed me. Lately, when he looked at me, his eyes weren't there, not with me.

Oh! I was tired of the emotional melodrama. If it weren't for the shutting me out, maybe I'd have had more patience for it. Early in our relationship, I had urged him to get his own place, but the urgency had dissipated; then we had both let it slide. Lately, we had been talking about it again, and this time, I was really pushing for him to do it, or at least for some kind of change. I couldn't go on the way we were . . . with him hardly even making eye contact. No. That was a kind of death. We definitely needed a change.

We were always breaking up and getting back together anyway. I thought it would be easier to figure out if we weren't actually living together. Maybe we just kept getting back together because we were sharing an apartment. It was hard to determine while we were still roommates.

Anyway, the drummer in his band had agreed to let him stay at his place, so the next day, Michael got up and started packing to move over there. I got dressed and went to the deli for our coffee.

When I returned, he was sitting on the couch, looking forlorn. I walked over, set the coffee on the coffee table, eased in on the couch behind him, and wrapped my arms around him. He lay back in my arms.

I asked, "Do you want me to cook you something?"

"No."

We both sat there in silence for a minute, then I said, "You know, Michael, when I got off work last night, part of me was hoping that you wouldn't be there, and the other part of me was hoping that you would be there—waiting for me, telling me that we can make it work—and that it will work."

He just lay there in my arms silent. I asked him, "Do you want me to make you some pasta? I could go get some meat."

"No."

We sat a little longer in silence; then I told him, "You can put some music on if you want."

He sipped his coffee, and started rummaging through the CDs . . . finally settled on a John Lee Hooker and put it in. I stood up and asked, "Can I use your green bag?"

"You can have my green bag," he said, as if nothing mattered anymore.

"You know where it is?"

"Either in the closet or by the desk."

He went into the closet and started pulling all of his clothes off the hangers and folding them, placing them on the ironing board.

Almost on the verge of tears, not feeling as sure about this as I had been before, I said, "I can't find the green bag. Do you know where it is?"

"Check by the desk."

Still not finding it, I picked up my big black bag, shoved a notebook and a couple of black pens into it, and threw it on my shoulder. I looked at him and said, "Well I wish you'd talk to me, but it's obvious you don't want to. You don't even want to look at me, so I'm going to the river."

He kept folding clothes in silence without looking at me, so I continued on, saying, "You know, Michael, I love you, but I just don't think we should be living together at this point. I don't like who I am with you right now. At the beginning, it seemed like we were stronger together. Like we inspired and admired each other. I don't just mean early infatuation stuff. It's like we were each a creative spark for the other. But something's gone wrong. We need our own place to get our perspective. If we're meant to be together, it will all work out anyway."

Finally breaking his silence, Michael jumped in with: "You know you're gonna have to come up with a better excuse than that. I know everything's not perfect, but we love each other. In your imagination, something's gone wrong . . . . You're gonna have to come up with something better than that."

"I didn't imagine that girl calling you here and a couple other things. I don't think I can trust you, and I don't think that's my imagination. Anyway, look, I'm going to the river. I need to clear my head. I hope you're here when I get back."

"We'll see."

I left my coffee on the table unopened. I didn't want it anymore anyway. Instead, I went back to the deli, got a big bottle of beer, and headed to the river.

When I got there, I sat down on my favorite bench, right next to the little statue of Ruthie the Duck Lady. I opened my beer and took a sip, then pulled out my notebook and started writing in it.

A homeless man walked up to me and said, "Hey! You writing your ole' man?"

I didn't answer.

He said, "Yeah," to no one in particular, "She's writin' her ole' man." Then he asked me, "You mind if I sit here and smoke a cigarette?"

Still writing and just quickly glancing up, I told him, "Actually, I'd prefer it if you didn't. I'm allergic to cigarette smoke." I'm not, but I was politely trying to send him off.

Undeterred, he said (again, to no one in particular), "Look at this beautiful lady. Yeah, she's writin' her ole' man and she's drinking Budweiser, and she has allergies and all." He finished smoking his Kool cigarette, then sat down next to me. I happened to be sitting in the middle of the bench. I didn't bother to move.

As he sat down he said, "Yeah, I like to sit down next to Ruthie too."

"You know her?" I asked, looking up.

"Everybody knows Ruthie. Well maybe not the new people. I probably knew Pops better though."

"Who's Pops?"

"He's dead now. Used to dance in the streets for tips. He was in love with Ruthie."

"Was she in love with him too?"

"Oh, I dunno. She used to say she was in love with someone else."

"Love is complicated."

"Are you in love?"

"Yes."

"Yeah, you're a beautiful lady and I know you love your ole' man. That's why you're writin' him. I know he loves you too. That's what it's all about. That's it. Love. That's all we got in this world."

With tears streaming down from underneath my sunglasses, I told him, "Look, now you've made me cry."

"That's okay. It's okay to cry. You let all that pressure build and it don't do you no good. That's okay now. Gotta let the pressure out."

Careful to replace the cap on my Budweiser after each sip, I asked him, "What's your name?"

"Joe. Hey, ya' gotta cigarette?"

"Sorry I don't smoke."

"Well, I could go buy me a pack if I wanted to. Ya' know I have money. I could buy me a pack."

I didn't say anything, just started writing again.

He said, "You're writing faster now. You must be goin' good. Tellin' your ole' man how you feel. You feel like you love him?"

"Yes I love him. I know he loves me too. That's not it," and I started crying again.

He said, "You know I was in love before—best feelin' in the world. Married her too."

I stopped crying and asked, "Are you still with her?"

"We were married sixteen years. Been separated four years. Three beautiful children too."

"How old are they?"

"They're all grown now."

"Still see them?"

"Oh yeah, see 'em all the time. They're doin' good. Real good."

"Why'd you split up?"

"She thought she was missin' something.' Thought she needed to go do her own thing. She comes and goes. Still see her sometimes."

"Well my boyfriend and I love each other, but I don't feel like I can trust him. Without trust, what can I do?"

"Well, you gotta do what you gotta do. I gotta go find a cigarette now, but I know you'll do all right. You'll do real good."

"Thanks! You will too."

Michael was gone when I got back, and I didn't call him, and he didn't call me. The next day, I went to the library to do some research on Pops and Ruthie. I don't know why. They had just really piqued my interest.

I found gobs of information on Ruthie. People had started buying photographs of her with her ducks when she was a young girl, and she had been a French Quarter attraction her entire life.

But all I found on Pops was a photo of him with his tongue sticking out. He was standing next to a tip box with a cardboard sign that said in shaky handwriting:

> Willie Taylor,
> i dance 69 years,
> i am 79 years old, i like,
> i love, The Duck Girl,
> Miss Ruthie, i love her 44
> years
> —soft shoe King of the
> United States of America.

Maybe they should put a little statue of him up next to her. I'd sit next to them.

I got some deli food on the way home and ate it out on my roof. I could see the river, but not the benches along the

Moonwalk, not the people sitting there or walking along. There was always someone there, although within a year, a month, a week, those benches hosted a wide range: tourists, homeless people, college kids from uptown branching out.

Not that long ago, I had been the bright young college kid. And look at me now: The day before, I had hung out on a bench down there, drinking beer and discussing my love life with a homeless man.

I felt caught between two worlds: I didn't feel like a local French Quarter boozer, but I blended in well, didn't I? In the past, I probably would have just brushed that homeless man off, as I had initially tried to do. Somehow, that didn't work anymore.

I finished my food, set the container inside the window, and sat out there a little longer. I thought of all the stories and all the people in the French Quarter and wondered how some of them found their way to—and inside of—me. It's curious how we open some books and not others.

Later, I headed over to Josephine's. It was pretty slow, but Josie and Matt were both there. I asked them about Pops and Ruthie.

Josie stopped what she was doing and said, "Pops used to come in here sometimes and someone would usually buy him a drink; otherwise I would. He drank CC and coke." She laughed and added, "When he found out my birthday was in September, he told me that his was too and asked me, 'What we is? Virgos?'"

Matt smiled and said, "I knew him too—and Ruthie. And a couple other interesting characters. But they're not around anymore."

I asked, "Where do old French Quarter characters go?"

Josie got me a drink and said, "I guess most of them live here until they die—if they're lucky."

Matt said, "Yeah, but there aren't that many anymore, not like Pops and Ruthie."

"Why do you think that is?"

"I'm not sure, but the French Quarter is changing, has changed; I can feel it—I can see it."

Josie said, "Yeah, but I think it will probably always attract eccentrics."

Matt asked for a refill then said, "Yes, but will they be able to afford to live here?"

Josie got his drink and said, "That's a good question. When I first moved here, everything was still cheap, and most places were dusty and semi-decrepit. Then things started changing. First, they spruced up Jax Brewery, then they brought in the Riverwalk and the Aquarium, then the casinos. Oh and the fancy lofts too."

"Shiny new places that don't accommodate dust or decay."

"The French Quarter seems to have gotten much more expensive too. Rents have gone way up."

Matt said, "Yeah, somewhere along the line, it's become a lot more high-dollar and a little less Bohemian."

Josie asked, "Are we the last of the Bohemian's, the end of an era?"

Matt said, "No, but we might be getting edged out. That's part of the reason the Faubourg Marigny has become more hip. Artists have moved over there and even up into Bywater."

I said, "Well maybe those areas have their Pops and Ruthie's."

Matt smiled and said, "Well, I don't care. It's the French Quarter for me. I will always find a way to live here."

As for me, I was staying, for the time being anyway. Would I grow up to be one of those old French Quarter characters? Probably not. I was a bird passing through, but sometimes I got wrapped up in it and forgot that a whole world existed outside of its borders.

20

Mambo Down in New Orleans

The previous Mardi Gras, I had taken off work and joined the festivities. This time, I probably would've done better if I had taken off work and left town. Instead, I worked the whole way through and experienced the full insanity: before work, trying to get to work, during work, and especially after work—trying to get home in the standstill pedestrian traffic as throngs of intoxicated tourists packed the streets shoulder to shoulder in an often-successful attempt to get females on balconies to show some skin.

There were people pissing, spitting, puking in doorways, and screaming just to test the limits of the lungs. I saw women showing big breasts and women showing flat chests; nobody seemed to discriminate either way. From the balconies, there were beads—and shrieks for more. There were people sleeping in cars, sleeping in doorways, sleeping on curbs, sleeping in Jackson Square, and sleeping in bars; the latter one often preceded puking. There was Lucky Dog breath everywhere! "Don't be a Meanie, buy her a weenie. Ten inches of fun in a bun!" The trash in both gutters was meeting each other. People drinking hurricanes were pissing and puking again. I actually saw sinks ripped out of bathrooms and doors ripped out of stalls. Signs were ripped off street posts, and holes were punched in the walls.

The last weekend of Mardi Gras was especially crazy. I was accustomed to working long hours with a high-volume crowd; however, these people were insane! Walking home after working a double, I could only sympathize with every cop I saw arresting a rowdy individual because, in my end-of-my-rope opinion, many of those people deserved to be incarcerated, or to at least be caged temporarily until the full moon waned.

Of course by that time, after serving those monsters ten hours for mere pennies, I had developed a serious attitude and was only waiting for someone to antagonize me so I could backhand them. Well, maybe. Normally I'm exceptionally passive and non-violent and had, in fact, never actually hit anyone in my entire life; however, I was feeling unusually provoked. I finally managed to make it home and didn't leave my apartment at all on Monday.

Michael came over and hibernated with me. After he had moved out, we'd decided that we couldn't live without one another and had been spending a lot of time together. He was present with me again. It was starting to feel like it had at the beginning. Although we weren't officially living together, he was spending most nights with me. Some of his stuff was even starting to make its way back over.

The next day was Fat Tuesday, and I worked from noon to six. My strategy was to avoid conflict, avoid confrontation, and avoid conversation. I may not have been entirely successful.

When I got to work, Jake asked if Michael and I had broken up. I looked at him with a *You've got to be kidding me* look on my face, and said, "Why do you ask?"

He didn't say anything right away, just looked flustered—and I knew. "You saw him with another woman, didn't you?"

"Uh . . . no, I thought it was him, but it was probably someone else. I'm sure it was someone else."

"And from the look on your face, Jake, I'm sure it was him."

He attempted, once more, to say that it probably wasn't, then walked away.

I was sick over it; I think my stomach and my chest traded places. I was mad too, and so was Erica when I told her. She always empathized with me. She was mad at Michael for doing me wrong and mad at Jake for not telling her right away. Anyway, we both got so very drunk—possibly in an attempt to numb the anger and shock—that we barely remember leaving. The entire time I worked there that's the only time that ever happened to me.

She went straight home and crashed. I thought I was going to go home, eat, and go back out—maybe uptown.

I went to the deli near my apartment for a hamburger. About that time, I blacked out. I vaguely remember telling the cook that I wanted the hamburger dressed. I don't remember if I tipped him, and I don't remember paying, or going home, or eating the hamburger; however, I'm assuming that all those things occurred.

The next thing I do remember is the King Cake. Hidden inside those things somewhere beneath the purple, green, and gold sugar is a plastic baby, and whoever gets it is supposed to host the next party or buy the next cake or whatever.

Anyway, I guess I had gotten one of those little miniature King Cakes at the deli. Apparently, I started eating it and—hey! I got the baby! That's what I remember: the icky feeling of biting into the plastic baby brought me back to conscious awareness of my environment for a few moments. Then I must have passed out.

I woke up when Erica called around 2 A.M. She had just woken up too. I told her, "I haven't been sleeping. I've merely been laying here unconscious for the past six hours or so in a drunken stupor."

"I guess I just clocked out and left?"

I laughed. "Wish I had. I hung out and visited with Roger for about five minutes; then I walked outside and talked to the bouncer next door for a little while. They must have known I was trashed."

I got off the phone with her and wrote in my journal, "Alcohol doesn't seem to be solving my problems, and it doesn't seem to be making them go away either. Damn, I was so hoping it would too! Au contraire, it only makes them seem to go away, temporarily, so that I put off dealing with them. Oh, how I sometimes love temporary!"

I concluded my journal entry by writing that it was the last time I was going to get drunk. *Yeah, right.*

When I got up the next morning, I still had all my make-up on, and the mascara on my eyelashes felt like dirty glue.

The part that really sucked was that I had to go to work that night. It's a bitch serving cocktails with a hangover. Drinking doesn't remedy the situation, but it helps. Finally, a double shot of Remy Martin made me feel better than the forty or so dashes of Bitters I'd been sucking down with Club Sodas.

I could feel heaviness and pressure on my chest. The muggy, damp weather with never-ending outbursts of rain wasn't helping either. I like the rain when I'm happy, but I hate it when I'm not. If I'm feeling sad, or anything like that, it just seems to totally intensify the feeling.

I really had the blues, and this time I couldn't find anything uplifting in it to take me to the other side.

Roger was there, but he didn't say anything about the night before. Either I had still been holding it together when I left, or he had decided to overlook it since it was the first time I'd ever been that bad off.

You might even say I was one of his favorite employees, although since he was so conservative and rigid it was hard to tell. Still, he had once told me, "If all the employees were like you, this place would run itself, and I wouldn't even have to show up." Maybe he didn't feel that way anymore. Oh well, I didn't care. I had other things to worry about.

Seth was bartending. I asked him, "Where does love fit into the search for the meaning of life?"

"Well, Samantha, everything is choice; nothing is mandatory. But if you're interested in pursuing love, it might be a good idea to love yourself first and make sure that you're always honest with yourself."

I gave a sad smile and said, "Love myself and be honest with myself? Sounds like that might be worth a try."

The conversation didn't cheer me up, but it did shake me out of the dark closet I had been hiding in, and it got me thinking. I'd been procrastinating in this stagnant pool of uncertainty long enough. It was time to do something.

21

The Truth

The next night, it was slow at work, so Roger let me off early. I decided to head home for a nice relaxing bath. As I went up the steps to my apartment, I noticed the door was slightly open, and I could hear Michael inside talking. That was a surprise because I wasn't expecting him to be there.

I walked lightly up the steps, pushed the door open quickly, and *No! I couldn't believe it.* Not that I hadn't suspected, but seeing is different than believing. It's more shocking and painful—and sad too . . . . He was sitting on the couch with his arm around a red-haired woman, the one I had seen at his gig one night. She was all curled in where I should have been! His other hand was holding hers, and she had obviously been crying.

I felt as if every cell in my body was being torn apart. There was fire raging through me, and I was melting. I wanted to scream; I wanted to pull her hair; I wanted to tell Michael to get the hell out.

I did none of those things. Instead, as Michael stood up and fumbled for words, and the woman sat there looking awkward, reaching for her purse, I just walked silently over to the French window, opened it, and climbed out onto the roof. I pulled my knees up to my chest and buried my head in my hands as I sank inside of myself, feeling very tiny and small, almost invisible, and sat there, still . . . .

The woman poked her head out and said, "For what it's worth, he loves you." She started crying and repeated, "He loves you," then turned and left.

Michael came out a moment later and said, "She's gone. Uh . . . you know, Sammi, that was nothing. We're just friends."

With all my strength, I slowly lifted my head and turned to look at him. I wasn't crying. I was kind of numb with shock at that point. Not that I had been clueless—but in my apartment while I was at work! That part I hadn't suspected.

As I looked into his eyes, he started fumbling for words again. I held my hand up and said, "No. Let's just be silent for a minute." And we just sat there for a few minutes, looking at each other, while our eyes talked.

Then I said calmly, "Tell me. I want you to tell me . . . the truth . . . today."

"I've been wanting to tell you the truth. I really have!"

"Here's your opportunity."

"I'm so sorry, baby! I wanted to be honest with you, but at the same time, I didn't want you to find out because I was afraid of losing you. It's over now. Completely. I *was* dating her for a little while, but that started when things between you and me were all messed up."

"What do you mean when things between you and me were all messed up? You started this before things were messed up. This is what messed things up."

"Yeah, but you were saying you didn't want to get married and that you would probably never marry me."

I could feel my heart starting to beat faster. Making a deliberate effort to still look and sound calm, I said, "Because I don't want to marry anybody. It's political bullshit! But I love you. And we were together because we wanted to be. Not because some piece of paper said that we were supposed to be—or had to be. "

"True."

"Well, see, when you got with this woman, you made another choice."

"She didn't mean anything to me, Sammi! The first time I was drunk. Then once I had already fucked up, everything was kind of messed up."

Running my fingers through my hair, I paused to grasp, clench, and pull hard, then I released and said, "Well see, even though I didn't have proof at the time, I knew that you were probably screwing around—not coming home until noon the next day sometimes . . . and that girl kept calling here."

"Why did you stay together with me then?"

"Because I love you. And I didn't have absolute proof. You always denied it and just told me that I was crazy. Sometimes I believed you. I couldn't break up with you on my suspicions. Besides, maybe you really loved me, and you were just going through some kind of phase."

"That's what I'm saying, baby. It took all that for me to realize how much I love you. I can't believe you're taking this so well, Sammi. I always wanted to talk to you openly like this, but I thought you'd get too upset. She didn't mean anything to me. I have *never* loved any woman the way I've loved you. You're the *only* one for me—the only one."

I had a sudden urge to bash my head through the wall, but I realized that would accomplish nothing useful. Instead, still trying to breathe and speak slowly, I told him, "That's what I thought: that maybe it was all nothing, you were just going through a hard time, or whatever; that's why you were distant. That you really loved me and that you'd come back around."

"That's what happened. I realize now what you mean to me."

"Now? I walked in on you—tonight—in *my* apartment—sitting on the couch with your arm around another woman," I said, no longer calm. "This was supposed to be *our* time, Michael, our love. Please, just leave my apartment! I don't want to see you again."

Tears started spilling out of his eyes. He reached over to hold my hands and said, "Sammi, the first time I got with her, I was very drunk and very stupid and very wrong. It would've been better if I could've been a man and come home and told you about it. Because what happened instead was I couldn't even look in your beautiful eyes anymore after that because I felt like shit, so that why I distanced myself from you. So then you and I weren't getting along well, and she was all over me, and since I had already messed up, it was easy to keep on keepin' on for a little while. But she meant nothing to me, and I realized how much you do mean to me, so tonight I was breaking it off completely. That's why she was crying."

"Well it's a little too late, and now I'm breaking it off completely with you. Please leave."

"Sammi!"

"I mean it. It's over."

He stood up, ran to the edge of our third-story roof—and jumped off! Shocked, I tried to look down without falling off myself. Alongside the parking meters, I could see cars lined bumper to bumper—but no Michael! I was horrified thinking that he had landed on one of the parked cars below and rolled off into the street.

I went inside and ran out the door and down the stairs as fast as I could, faster maybe.

As I reached the sidewalk, he came running up. I think we were both so relieved he was okay that we both just started laughing hysterically. Miraculously, he had not landed on a car and had not been hurt in any way. He just felt a little jarred.

For a moment, I thought about taking his hand and bringing him back up to my apartment to make up, to just do our best to forget about the whole thing, to wipe the slate clean.

But no! I couldn't, I didn't, I wouldn't. He had taken his leap of faith and survived. Walking away from him—even as every cell in my body wanted to take him into my arms and hold him—be with him—walking away in spite of that was *my* leap of faith . . . or maybe it was my ticket to freedom. After the shock of the whole thing wore off, I told him goodbye and went back upstairs.

My intuition was right; my suspicions were justified. I wasn't crazy or irrational or insanely jealous after all. I had looked so calm as he told me, so calm as I listened, so calm as I sat there unable to breathe. And the truth came out, and although it was upsetting and maybe even a little scary, it did make me feel better.

I had felt weak, dependent, and insecure up until that night. Those feelings were all gone now. I felt powerful again. I was taking back, or reclaiming, my power.

When I got back upstairs, I looked around the apartment at all our memories. I started grabbing everything of his and throwing it into a pile. I suddenly remembered a movie I had seen where the scorned woman threw all the cheating man's stuff out the window.

Oh, and Dana too. According to Dana, she had once put the entire wardrobe of an ex-who-had-done-her-wrong into the bathtub and set it on fire—while making him watch. According to her, he deserved it. Not that he could say much about it because she had paid for all of his clothes anyway. At any rate, he never bothered her again.

I thought about doing something destructive to Michael's stuff for a millisecond, but that just wasn't me. Besides, he'd probably end up asking to borrow money from me to replace any missing items, and I'd probably lend it to him. *Oh, that beautiful foolish boy!*

My immediate plan of action was to eliminate him entirely from my life. No phone calls, no visits, no contact.

I had the next two nights off, during which I just stayed inside my apartment and hibernated and avoided everybody. I needed some time alone to process everything before I had any human contact.

Not only did I have to fight the urge to contact Michael or to pick up the phone the numerous times that he called, I also had to fight the urge to contact any of my friends until I was definite about going through with this breakup because I didn't want to embarrass myself by publicly changing my mind about it later. But after two nights in my enclave, I finally emerged from my apartment and glided through the Quarter and into work. I was ready.

Katie told me, "Hi. You ready for a drink?"

I smiled. "Do you have to ask?"

When she brought it over, she said, "We're going to Nugent's after work. Come with us."

I took a sip and said, "I think I will. Michael and I broke up—for good this time, and I really should go celebrate."

"Samantha! You just slip these things into casual conversation! That's such big news. And I never would have guessed! You came in like you were in a good mood tonight."

"I don't know if I'm in a good mood exactly, but we've been heading toward breaking up for so long now that I'm glad it's finally over. It's a relief almost."

Erica came over then, and Katie said, "Samantha and Michael broke up!" So of course Erica asked me what happened too.

I told her, "I really don't want to talk about it right now. It's just over. Completely this time."

"You found out for sure, didn't you?"

"Lucky guess."

"Well, when you feel like talking, you know I'm here for you."

We made it through the night and headed over to Nugent's. Katie insisted on buying me a drink and asked, "So how are you doing?"

I told her, "I'm fine, really. I don't want to go into all the stupid little details. Let's just never mention his name again."

"I don't even remember it," she said with a smile.

"That's what I'm talking about."

"Let me just say, we always thought you could do better."

"Thanks. Maybe next time I will."

A couple of drinks later, I decided I did want to talk about it, but not to them for some reason. I didn't want everyone at work to know every detail about my life—not right then anyway, not until I had enough emotional distance to discuss it in an amusing and witty way. I told them goodbye and headed over to Josephine's.

With Josie, I could talk about anything and everything. Josie was my priest.

After she brought me my drink, I told her that I finally had proof of Michael's cheating and that he had admitted it.

"And you let him live?"

I laughed and said, "Here's the thing: I refuse to sit around and blame anybody for anything. In my subconscious, I've known for some time, but for whatever reason I just wasn't ready to break up with him until now. So now I found out for sure, made the decision, and followed through. Or at least I'm in the process of following through."

"That's a mature way of looking at it."

"Well it's the truth. He and I had fun for a while, but that's all it was. We tried to make it more serious than that and drag all this heartbreak melodrama into it, when really we should have broken up long ago, or maybe never have even gotten together. But no, we did fit together for a little while . . . and some parts were really good. It's just time to move on."

"Yeah, when it's not fun anymore, it's time to move on. Unless you're married, but that's an entirely different story. You're supposed to see it through in that scenario."

"Do you want to get married?"

"Oh God no! At least not for a long, long time. I have a lot of things I want to do before then. A lot of places I want to go."

"Me too. Hey, maybe I'll move to Key West and marry some Hemingway wannabe. Or, better yet, maybe I'll be the Hemingway wannabe."

"Have you ever been to Key West, Samantha?"

"No, why?"

"It's full of beautiful boys. Granted a lot of those boys have grey hair. They all seem to have a lack of ambition in common."

"Hmmm. Cute, immature boys . . . I probably don't have to go all the way to Key West for that."

"I wouldn't think so. But it all depends on what you're looking for. It can be fun. The most bizarre thing was that every guy I slept with there read Bukowski to me before sex."

I laughed and asked, "*Every* guy you slept with?"

"Okay, there were only two. But it turned out that they didn't even know each other, so that Bukowski-as-seduction thing must have been really widespread."

"Must've been. Oh well, maybe I'll skip Key West and head out to California. At least there I can attempt to expand my mind."

"Even more than it already is?"

"The possibilities are limitless."

"Hey, how about Europe?"

"I've always wanted to go there."

"Me too! I don't know if I'll ever make it there or not, but I might."

"Where would you go?"

"I'd like to stay in Paris for at least a month and see if I could find some way to live there."

"Yes, Josie, I could totally see you in Paris."

"How about you? Where would you go?"

"I don't know. I actually speak a few languages, so I could probably go just about anywhere. I might get a Eurail pass and see as much as I can, then decide where I want to go from there."

"Do you seriously think you might do it?"

"Well I know I would love to, but I never seem to be able to make or save enough money. I'm thinking maybe I could go to either San Francisco or New York first and make some money there, then go."

The sun was almost up by then, so I told her bye, headed home, and went to sleep as the first morning rays came through the window. A few hours later, the phone rang and woke me up. It was Bianca.

I told her all the latest news. She grunted. "How heartbreaking! The scoundrel!"

"In a way it is all very heartbreaking, but in another way, it's very liberating. Like now I can go anywhere I want to go and do anything I want to do. I used to feel that way, but after things started to get messed up with Michael, it wasn't like that anymore. I was missing that."

"Well then, his philandering and lies have set you free. And I thought it was love that's supposed to set you free."

"Well, insecurity and inconsistency don't. Anyway, I don't have any commitments right now—no romance, no career. My lease is almost up at my apartment, and all I need to extricate myself from The Blue is a two-week notice."

"So are you really going to quit?"

"Well not yet. It's just something I'm thinking about. I'm trying to look at all my options right now."

"What options are you considering?"

"Oh, they change from moment to moment. I know I could go back to school if I wanted, and even go on to law school. Then what? Stay in one place and be a lawyer for the rest of my life?"

"You certainly could if you wanted to . . . but the way you describe it makes it sound like a marriage."

"Like something I'm not ready for yet—if ever."

"Exactly."

"I think I still have some wanderlust in me. I'm much more excited about taking off and changing my destiny with a plane ticket—or a bus ticket, depending on the money situation."

"So where are you thinking about going?"

"Oh I probably won't go anywhere, but I'm playing with the idea of going to either San Francisco or New York."

"Either one would be exciting, I'm sure."

"In the meantime, I'm just going to hang out here—keep working at The Blue, and maybe discover what it's like to be single in the Quarter."

"Well good because I want to come see you. For my graduation present to myself, I'm going to take a cross-country road trip and maybe do some interviews along the way. I'll be passing right through New Orleans, so I want to stop by for a visit."

"Graduation? You're graduating?"

"Yes, finally. I tried to hold off and wait for you, but this was about as long as I could stretch it."

"Well I'd love to see you. Come on down. I'll show you around."

"I'm looking forward to it. I want to see the city that stole you away from a life like mine."

"It's a state of mind."

"No state of mine."

"Well come on down. Maybe it will take you too."

"Take me where?"

"Wherever you want to go."

"Sounds fun. See you soon!"

After I got off the phone with her, the doorbell rang. I had a doorbell, but no intercom, and the buzzer to buzz people in was broken. So after one of my friends would ring the bell, they knew to step across the street so that we could yell back and forth through the French windows. Then, if need be, I could run downstairs and let them in.

I opened the window and looked down to see who it was. Michael was standing across the street with some purple iris flowers, my favorite. I shook my head but told him, "Be right down," against my better judgment.

I glanced in the full-length to see how I looked: ponytail, shorts, and a tank top. I actually looked good. Too good. I quickly slipped out of that and into a sundress, then went down to see what he wanted.

"Open the gate, and let me in so we can talk."

"We can talk right here, through the gate."

"Please, Sammi, let me in. We can just sit in the courtyard and talk."

Soon as I got the door open, he squished in, wrapped his arms around me, and said, "Baby, please don't cut me loose—I need you in my life!"

I pulled away from him and headed over to a little bench in the courtyard as I quietly answered, "It's not going to work Michael." I almost felt as if I meant it too . . . at least in that moment I did . . . almost.

He followed, sat down next to me, and asked, "Are you pushing me out of your life completely?"

"I thought that was clear. Can you give me a good reason not to?" He opened his mouth to speak, and I said, "No forget it. Don't even bother."

He looked down, then put his head in his hands. Neither one of us said anything for a few minutes. We just sat there in silence, during which time, I resisted the urge to stroke the back of his neck . . . or any other part of him.

Finally, he looked up and said, "You know, Sammi, we edge people out of our lives for various reasons. Often times, they've crossed one of our lines, one of our personal boundaries, and we no longer permit them to associate with us in any way."

"That's pretty much what's happened here," I said, turning my face away.

He reached over, gently put his fingers on my chin, and guided it back to face him as he said, "Yes, maybe, but most of the time though, if we're completely honest, there's at least one thing we still like about that person. Maybe they made us laugh, or they were an intellectual match or a spiritual match, or maybe they were just fun to hang out with. Surely there's at least one thing you still like about me."

"Yes. You and I had some kind of a connection, Michael, but that's over now."

He slid his fingers around to the back of my neck, started gently stroking my hair, and said, "Does it have to be, Sammi? Do we have to cut people out of our lives entirely when they cross the line? I think it would be better if we could keep people in our lives for the things that we like about them, and not have to kick them out for the things that we don't like. You know, not expecting any one person to offer all of the qualities that we are looking for in a person."

Naturally I wasn't immune to his charms and felt as I were about to surrender into them, so I stood up to put some distance between us and told him, "You make a lovely idealist or philosopher, Michael, even a lovely lover, but a lousy boyfriend. I don't know how to transition from what I thought we were supposed to be to what we are now.

Furthermore, I don't think I even want to. If it weren't for the lies, maybe."

"I'm human. I make mistakes. I can change. If I had some kind of commitment from you, I could change."

"Yes, well, that's not going to happen. But I do find your bit about no *one* person being our *everything* interesting. That we can like people for different reasons, or maybe just one or two reasons. I'll keep that in mind in my future relationships. It's too late for us though. I'm closing this chapter."

But I didn't . . . .

22
Mojo Workin'

After Michael and I broke up, I started feeling changes taking place inside of me. I was craving salt more, as well as the smell of incense. It also seemed as if I could smell more clearly, and I was able to distinguish more between different smells.

I was suddenly able to see how much of my life essence that I used to give to Michael. Now that I wasn't worrying about him all the time, I started thinking about what I could do, what *I* had to offer. The less I saw of him, the more I seemed to have an excess of energy and agape love which I could feel pouring out of me, and I needed to direct that energy somewhere.

I was really feeling that way one night, so I went to A&P and got a couple of loaves of bread and some lunchmeat. I went home and made up some huge triple-decker sandwiches, then walked around the French Quarter handing them out to homeless people. I'd stop and ask one, "Hey buddy, are you hungry?" Then I'd hand him a sandwich and walk on.

One was sleeping at a stoop on Decatur. I tapped him with my foot and asked if he wanted a sandwich. When he looked up at me, I noticed that he was the same man

Roger had kicked out of The Blue one night, the one who had said that he used to be a millionaire movie producer.

He just reached up for the sandwich and said, "Thanks."

I told him, "You're welcome," and moved on.

I moved on, or was in the process of moving on anyway, but he hadn't. Had he really once been a millionaire movie producer who set it all aside to do research for a book on homeless people, or was he merely a homeless person with illusions of grandeur that he could someday become a millionaire movie producer?

Whichever one he was, or had been, or would someday become, one thing was certain: that night he was just another hungry homeless person in the French Quarter. I didn't know why he was there, and I couldn't drastically change his circumstances in any way; however, for one night, I could feed him.

Did that one sandwich that one night make a difference in his life? Probably not. But I think, somehow, it made a difference in mine. To me, he was the epitome of how a person can get stuck at a certain point in their life and get trapped in a tunnel where they can't see a way out, or even worse, they forget that there is any other way. I had been that way for a while. I didn't want to be anymore. And for some reason, seeing him reminded me that I didn't have to be. I wished there was a way that I could have reminded him, but I didn't know how. I was just barely remembering myself. The only thing I knew to do was to hand him that sandwich.

The next night I was supposed to be off, but Erica asked me to work for her. I told her I would because I didn't even know what I was in the mood for, so I figured I might as well make a little money.

Some new girls were working, but at least I had Seth to talk to. I told him about the breakup and that I had hardly been able to sleep since, and besides, I just didn't feel like going home that night.

He said, "You could come to my place," then quickly added, "You don't have to worry about me. I'm celibate."

I raised my eyebrows. "I know what that means, but I never heard anyone say it before . . . not like that."

"Like it's a choice?"

"Exactly."

"Well, I'm not a virgin, and I have been in love before. It's just that at this stage in my life—or in my evolution or development, I'm choosing not to go that route. It's kind of liberating actually. I can be friends with whoever I want to be friends with, and spend time with whoever I want, and even love whoever I want to, without getting confused or misdirected by romantic love—via sex."

"And see? Now you've totally persuaded me to come home with you when I probably otherwise wouldn't have."

"See how liberating celibacy is?"

"You make it sound kind of cool."

We walked over to his efficiency apartment on Dauphine Street. It was simple and functional. We visited for a few minutes; then he offered me a massage.

I said, "Sure, that'd be great," thinking he meant a shoulder rub.

He opened the closet, got a massage table out, and set it all up. Then he put on some relaxing music.

"Wow. So you meant a real massage."

"Yeah, I studied it out in California and actually did it for a living for a while, but I decided I didn't like doing it as a job. So now, I bartend or whatever for a living, but I massage whoever I want to, whenever I want to."

I smiled. "So I guess today's my lucky day. I never got a real massage before. What do I do?"

"You don't have to remove any clothes if you don't want to, or you can strip down to your underwear. But I'll have a sheet over you, and all private parts will be completely covered at all times."

"Then I accept."

As he started massaging my head, my neck, my shoulders, my back, I—the forever insomniac, relaxed completely and began to drift off—not to sleep actually, but somewhere else, somewhere between being asleep and being awake.

It was almost as if every part of my body had a memory, and as he touched each part, it awakened that memory, or maybe that dream.

I felt as if I were everywhere at once, but at the same time, I felt as if I were more whole and solid than I had ever been before—I was just big: really, really big. Bigger than the room, bigger than the city. Bigger than the world maybe.

When I woke up, sunlight was streaming in through the windows, and I was still lying on the massage table.

Seth was sitting on the floor reading. As I looked at him, he set his book down and asked, "How do you feel?"

I stretched my toes and my ankles. "I feel like I just got the best night's sleep I ever had in my life—or maybe the *only* night's sleep I ever had in my life!"

"Would you like some Ginseng tea?"

"I don't even know what that is, but sure. Sounds great."

He came back a few minutes later with the tea and some yogurt with granola. We ate it sitting against two big pillows on the floor.

I told him, "Some day maybe I'll choose to be as healthy as you are."

He grinned. "It is about choice. You have what you choose when you choose it. Even now. When you choose something different, you'll have something different."

"So why did you choose to stop drinking?"

"Because I did that for as long as I wanted to, then I didn't want to anymore. If I want to again, I will. But right now, today, that's not the me that I want and choose to be."

I looked at him strangely for a moment, then asked, "What are *you* doing in the French Quarter?"

"Just passing through. Believe it or not, the French Quarter is cool even for people who don't drink. I probably won't be here much longer though.. At this phase in my life, I like to participate in a community short term, without getting enmeshed in society. Being a traveler allows me to do that. When I get tired of it, I'll stop."

"Where will you go next?"

"I don't know yet. I'll be here until I do."

"Well I'm glad to know you, Seth. Even if it's just for a little while."

Before leaving, I glanced at some of his books. I had been an avid reader all my life, but I didn't recognize any of the titles on his shelf. He pulled down *The Celestine Prophecy* by James Redfield and lent it to me, saying that it might help explain why we meet the people we do. Then he gave me a ride home.

I went upstairs and looked around, somehow seeing the space with new eyes, after being in someone else's place. There was a hole in the wall where one of Michael's vintage guitars used to hang. I could have just filled the hole in—as if to pretend it had never been there, but instead, I decided to create something of my own for that space.

I went and bought some supplies from a local art shop and painted a picture to hang there. On my third try, I got it to look almost the same as the picture I had in my mind. It was my version of the Mississippi river as it brushed up against the French Quarter. It wasn't an accurate portrayal, and the colors were a little brighter, but you could tell what it was.

Even though I wasn't an artist and it wasn't the most beautiful painting in the world, it made me happy to see it hanging there, in the space that used to hold something else. Somehow, it reminded me—or helped me to realize— that there is no true loss, only change. We just rearrange. The seeming absence of one thing makes room for something else.

My life, however, didn't suddenly transform and mesh into constant peace and love; there was still a nervousness in it too. I wasn't used to sleeping alone. I just couldn't seem to drop off, and when I finally did, my dreams took the shapes of terrifying worst-case scenarios.

Not only that, but I also started hearing really loud and strange noises in my apartment. One night, I had just lain down to go to sleep—I was actually sober too—and I looked at the time on the clock, then closed my eyes. Right away, I heard a sound directly behind my head, close to my ear. It sounded like a wild animal snarling. I opened my eyes and only one minute had passed on the clock. I hadn't dozed off—I had been awake!

I wanted to get out of my apartment immediately, but I was paralyzed in my terror. Then, through tremendous will power, or maybe just a huge surge of adrenaline, I bolted out of bed, flew to the door, and ran out on the stairwell. Since I wasn't dressed, I couldn't go anywhere immediately. I just sat out there, naked on the stairs, until my heart quit beating halfway out of my chest. Fortunately, no one else could see me. Since it was an attic apartment, the stairwell led only to my door.

I deduced: Either the sound had been real, or I was going crazy. Neither scenario sounded good to me.

When I finally calmed down enough, I went back inside, leaving the door open in case anyone needed to hear my screams. I grabbed the clothes I had been wearing earlier, which were conveniently lying on the floor, right next to the door. I was more grateful than ever for my poor housekeeping skills.

I dressed in the stairwell, headed to The Abbey, and didn't come home until daylight. Daylight was safe. Daylight was pure. Nothing bad ever happened in the daylight.

Hemingway had described it perfectly for me: "I know the night is not the same as the day: that all things are different, that the things of the night cannot be explained in the day, because they do not then exist . . . ."

I slept for a couple of hours, then got up and figured a few things out. I called our karate instructor to tell him that Michael and I had broken up and that I would no longer be attending class. We talked for a while, and I vaguely mentioned the strange things that had been taking place in my apartment.

He told me that it sounded like voodoo, that he would help me if I wanted, that there were things we could do to protect me and my environment, and not only that, there were also things we could do to smooth things out between Michael and me, to turn him into my loyal little puppy dog, so to speak.

I told him that I wasn't interested in using voodoo. He warned me that if Michael had used voodoo on me that I would probably find it necessary to use some too—to at least protect myself.

I thanked him and hung up, with no intention of ever calling him again. I knew that he was powerful, I just couldn't be entirely positive that he was on my side. Because Michael and I had spent an equal amount of time with him, I didn't know where his loyalties lay, although they were probably with me. I just couldn't be sure who to trust at that point.

I called Josie to talk to her about it. She told me, "I'm just about to head into work. Come see me there."

"I thought that other guy was working tonight."

"Uh . . . yeah, that didn't work out. It *is* hard to find good help. Do you want to come work for me?"

"Oh I'm definitely not good help. Besides, I prefer sitting on the other side of your bar, and I wouldn't want to mess that up."

She laughed and said, "Well meet me there. I'll save your stool."

When I arrived, there were only two other people there, so Josie and I were able to talk. I told her about the strange events and about what my karate instructor had said, then asked her, "What is voodoo anyway?"

"Magic. Some people call it black magic. Maybe it incorporates white magic too. I really don't know."

"Do you think the stuff going on at my place could be voodoo? Do you believe in that stuff?"

"I don't know, Samantha. I've seen some stuff—scary stuff—that I can't discount it completely."

Matt came in at that point, and I filled him in on what we had been talking about, while Josie went to refill her other customers.

He asked me, "Do you believe in telekinesis?"

"That people can move things with their minds?"

"Yes."

"I definitely believe it's possible, but I don't have absolute proof because I've never actually done it myself . . . well, not while I'm awake."

He smiled and asked, "You've done it in your sleep?"

"A couple of times."

"Me too!"

Josie came back and got us refills, but the bar was starting to fill up, so she had to go take care of her customers. Before leaving, she said, "I always miss all the good conversations."

I told her, "Now you see why I don't want to work here."

After she walked away, Matt went on, asking, "And have you heard that there are some people, currently living, who have been able to manifest solid objects out of thin air?"

"You mean like Yogi Masters?"

"Yes. But what if we were all capable of that—the manifesting of solid objects and the telekinesis? What if we all *are* capable of that, and maybe we just don't know it yet, or don't remember how to do it?"

"Oh, okay, I see where you're going. And what if we could all use those powers for either positive or negative. Well then, the negative might not really be evil; it might just be like a scary movie somebody produced."

"Exactly! Personally, Samantha, I don't believe that any of that stuff taking place at your apartment will physically hurt you. I believe it's just a movie meant to scare you. Maybe so you won't want to be alone anymore. Maybe you'd even get scared enough to want to take Michael back. See?"

"Oh yes. That makes so much sense! I still want it to stop though."

"I have faith in you. You'll find a way."

Two days later, Michael came over and brought my favorite and most frequently worn black skirt, which I had not been able to find, as well as a hair clip that I often wore. He had come over when I wasn't there and had taken those items—without my knowledge—to—of all people—the Chicken Man! The Chicken Man! He was some sort of voodoo king.

Then he started telling me some of my adventure one day, details about which nobody could have known, well nobody in the French Quarter anyway.

I had ventured out, taken the streetcar uptown, and to my knowledge, there had been no witnesses. I went to the library on St. Charles, hung out there for a while, then went over to Tulane University to check out the campus. Ended up having a beer or two in the pub, may have even flirted with some college boy too. Some little bitty fling there. We had gotten into a discussion about John Kennedy Toole's *Confederacy of Dunces*, and he had taken me back to his dorm room to read some excerpts—his dorm room! Really it was just a brief escape from missing Michael. On the way home, I had stopped off at Whole Foods.

Not a big deal, but how could anybody else have known? Someone might have seen me at one of those locations, but no one could have seen me at all three, unless they had followed me. Highly unlikely since they were in three different directions. Apparently, the Chicken Man had held my items, then relayed the scenes to Michael as if he were seeing them on a TV screen.

Naturally, I demanded—and got—my apartment key back from Michael right then. I didn't tell him about the snarling incident or any of the other strange stuff that had been going on because if he had, and I was quite sure that he had, asked the Chicken Man to inflict some type of voodoo on me, I didn't want him to know that it was working. I would have to either take my own measures to protect myself, or leave town altogether.

A little while after he left, I decided to go to the river. I walked over behind the French Market, went up the steps on one side of the wall and down the steps on the other side, ran across the tracks right before a streetcar went by, and went over to my favorite bench on the Moonwalk.

I stayed out there for about an hour, staring out at the ripples in the water and contemplating life. I couldn't believe Michael had taken my stuff to the voodoo man! I still felt that I had done the right thing turning my karate instructor down, but I needed to do something—I just didn't know what.

I got up, headed over to Decatur Street, and started walking toward the French Market. There was a guy across the street who sometimes read tarot cards in Jackson Square. I had also seen him hanging out at Molly's and at The Abbey a couple of times. He had a pair of oriental exercise balls that he was manipulating in a circular path in one of his hands. He always had them with him.

I crossed over and asked him where I could get a pair. He told me that he had gotten them at the French Market; then he showed me how to do them. Naturally, I wasn't as good as he was on my first try; however, I understood the concept.

He complimented me and said, "You're Michael's girlfriend, aren't you?"

"No, actually we broke up."

"Good! I can't stand that son of a bitch." He grabbed my hand and said, "My name's Dominic. Come with me to The Abbey, and you can tell me all about it."

I laughed and let him pull me in. As soon as we sat down, two kamikazes were placed in front of us, and as soon as we drank them, they were replaced with another and another. Some guy kept sending rounds to everyone; then he bought a pizza from across the street and shared that too.

At some point, Dominic spread his tarot deck out on the bar, gave me a complimentary reading, and answered three questions. One of the cards showed that there was some type of division occurring in my life at that point, and another showed that I would soon be taking a long journey by myself.

I told him, "I don't know if it's the tarot cards or just your natural psychic ability coming through, but if I had known you were so intuitive, I might have consulted you earlier."

He smiled. "Feel free to consult me anytime. It's my pleasure to spend time with you."

"Thanks Dominic. I normally don't ask anybody for advice or guidance. I tend to muddle through blindly by myself until finally I can see the light."

"Sometimes that's the best way to find it. Anyway, that's part of your natural charm: your strong independent streak. It's part of your nature. Allen Ginsberg said, 'Follow your inner moonlight; don't hide the madness.' Don't apologize for it. Embrace it and go with it."

I smiled and quoted Emerson, saying, "The Sphinx must solve her own riddle."

I figured only in New Orleans could I be sitting in a bar in the middle of the afternoon, a crowded bar at that, having some man read my tarot cards, and nobody even seemed to notice. Well, at least it was Friday. Nevertheless, I could walk in there any day of the week and it would usually be just as crowded.

I told him about all the nightmares I had been having and the other stuff that had been going on. He told me not to worry, that he would help me take care of it. He said that he would do something about it, and he also gave instructions for me to do that included using incense, salt, and repeating a couple of phrases.

I told him, "That's really odd because lately I've suddenly been craving salt and the smell of incense."

"Most of the time we intuitively know what we need if we just pay attention."

I left there and went on to the French Market. Even though there were some touristy things there, it had actually been a market since the 1800's, maybe even earlier than that, and was originally just a place for the locals to do their shopping.

That's what it was for me. If I wanted an avocado, or a cucumber, or a Halloween pumpkin, or a Christmas tree (or a prescription for some disturbing dreams), that's where I went. Of course if a tourist wanted gourmet sauces, or alligator on a stick, or an eel skin wallet, or some tee shirts, they could get those things there too.

There was a sign at the entrance that said: "Quality is like buying oats. If you want good clean oats, you must pay a fair price. If, however, you are satisfied with oats after they have already passed through the horse, well then, they are a little cheaper." It was appropriate for the French Market too because you could find things from both ends there.

Anyway, I made my purchases, including some oriental exercise balls, then I went home and did the things that Dominic had suggested. I don't know if the instructions he gave me were just designed to have a sugar-pill, panacea effect, to calm me down and make me feel like I was doing something, but I did them anyway.

That night, I discovered that my fear was indeed gone, along with the strange noises. But that uncovered what was left—my loneliness. It was still weird being alone in my bed. I climbed in, but it took me a long time to fall asleep.

23

New Lovers

I knew it wouldn't take him long, and I was counting on that too, but shit! It had only been two weeks since the break-up, and I already saw Michael walking openly down the street with another girl. Funny, she looked like me too. Was that intentional?

All in all, it was a relief, because finally I knew that, once and for all, it was over. Well, probably anyway. That is exactly what I wanted. All the same, I didn't know that it would feel so awkward and sad. Yes, Michael and I had split up completely, and the next time he came over, I would remind him of that. And the time after that too . . . .

As angry and as hurt as I was, I was still deeply attracted to him, which made it difficult for me to send him away.

So I usually didn't.

Sure I melted at his touch, but that wasn't it. All he had to do was say my name—there was something about the way he said it—and I was compelled to spend a few borrowed hours with him . . . until my logical sensibilities, resentment toward him, and sometimes even disgust returned. But the next time he'd say my name, that would all melt away again, along with all ability to think and reason . . . for a few hours anyway.

He came over a few days later to try to talk me into getting back together with him. After some blissful passion, we were sitting on the couch talking, and he told me, "You seem so much stronger and independent now, more like you were when I first met you."

He would have done better if he hadn't remind me of that—nothing like reality to bring me back to my senses. I turned slightly, put my feet up on the coffee table, and said, "That's because I'm getting back what I gradually lost while I was with you. Anyway, I saw you with your new girl the other day."

He leaned forward trying to reestablish eye contact and said, "She was a friend—that's it. You're the *only* one I want, baby! I don't need anyone else. I made my mistake and now I can see how important you are to me. All I need is *you*!"

I covered my eyes with my hands and said, "I don't even think I want to have this fling thing with you anymore, Michael. I don't think it's working out."

He pulled my hands off my eyes and said, "I don't want a fling with you, Sammi. I love you! I could probably even marry you. You're the one who never wanted to talk about getting married."

I looked at him directly and said, "Damn it, Michael. I really love you. Damn you for screwing this up!"

Although I was definitely not over him, I did start to move on after that. A little bit anyway. I wasn't riding in his wake anymore, or arranging my day and night and life around his. I was stepping out in my own direction, and it felt good.

Matt talked me into going with him to a poetry reading in the Faubourg Marigny. After signing in, we sat down at a table near the front, and I got us some drinks.

When it was his turn, Matt went up there and did some clever little haiku that was over almost as soon as it started. A round of surprised laughter and applause followed.

Then it was my turn. I walked up there with weak legs and a pounding heart. I managed to make it to the stool somehow and sat down. I was just silent for a minute, and surprisingly, so was the audience. Then, once I started reciting, fortunately, my voice was steady and calm and everything I wanted it to be.

Afterward, I went and sat back down and reached for my drink. Matt said, "You did great! You didn't even seem nervous. Were you?"

I finished my drink and set it down. "Well, the funny thing is that I *was* nervous right before, but as soon as I got up there and sat on the stool, I was fine. It was no big deal."

The manager came over at that point, sat down, and talked with us for a few minutes. He already knew Matt, so they talked first; then he turned to me and told me that my poem was well received and asked if I had any more.

"Selective handfuls."

"Would you come back and read again sometime?"

"I'd be delighted."

He said, "Great. I look forward to seeing you again." He told the bartender to buy us another round, then he walked off to work the room.

Matt set his empty glass down and motioned to mine: "Do you want another one?"

"Sure, sounds good."

Just then, Matthew Nolan, a local well known poet, came up and complimented us on our poems and handed us each a shot of Jagermeister. After he left, Matt and I started talking about maybe reading some of our collaborations together sometime.

I told him, "Too bad poets don't really make any money to begin with. Since we write together, we'd have to split *nothing* in half."

"At least we get a free drink now and then."

Some other people came over and talked to us, and the whole experience was very affirming. I felt like a real person there, like an individual again, worthy in my own right. I wasn't just a pretty face or just Michael's girlfriend there. No one even knew or cared who he was. They actually liked me for what I had to say.

It wasn't the first time I had ever felt like that, but it was the first time I had felt that way in a long time.

So . . . I certainly wasn't in any hurry to find a replacement for Michael. I was enjoying my own company. Nevertheless, I did find myself a lover anyway. I didn't set out to do it, and really, the guy I chose wasn't even my type. But that was better really. I wasn't looking for my type.

I woke up around 2:30 Sunday afternoon. Some band was playing at Spanish Plaza Riverwalk from four to eight, so I took a shower, got dressed, and headed over.

When I arrived, the band was just starting. They were mainly doing New Orleans music, which I adore, but I also remember they did some song about variety being the spice of life, which must have planted a seed in my head or inspired me in some way. I was already feeling open to anything anyway.

I saw two girls dancing up on a high wall, so I went and joined them, and we were immediately the best of friends. After a cop made us get down, we headed up to the front of the stage and started dancing there.

That's when I ran into the old man, the one who reminded me of my grandfather. He and I were the only two people I knew who made it to every single festival held in the general French Quarter area (as if it were our job or something), and we would always dance, so dance we did.

At one point, the band asked for volunteers to come up on the stage to do some dance I had never heard of before. Nevertheless, I was one of the first volunteers up there—doing my own dance; I always did my own dance. The two girls I had been dancing with were up there too, plus a couple of other people: about eight of us altogether, but I was right up front, dancing with the lead singer of the band.

Anyway, as I got off the stage, I ran into Ethan, the lawyer who had gotten my case expunged. Or maybe he ran into me. He had apparently seen me dancing up there and had made his way over.

He reached for my hand to help me down and said, "Uh, hi. Do you remember me?"

I smiled. "Yes, Ethan. I remember you." I pulled him in a little closer, and said, "This is actually a very good time for you to run into me—I'm single now."

He grinned. I think he may have even blushed.

Although he was attractive and a very nice guy, he was, under normal circumstances, entirely not my type: light hair and perfect. He came across as very appropriate. I usually went for a little more character and creativity in appearance and style.

Nevertheless, he and I hung out the rest of the night, and somehow I ended up getting into his car with him and going back to his place.

He was a perfect gentleman. He seated me on the couch and served me wine in a wine glass. Even though he'd had no idea that I would be coming over, his apartment was immaculate. I got the feeling that it always looked that way.

I told him, "Just to let you know, you're a rebound fling. I'm not over my ex-boyfriend yet."

He smiled. "I'm okay with that. Whatever I can do to help make your life easier and more pleasant, you just let me know."

But, as it turned out, he wasn't just a one-date diversion. He was along for the ride, as far as it would go. Jazz Fest started the next weekend, and we went together.

As we walked up to the entrance, he told me, "I love Jazz Fest. I think it's my favorite event in New Orleans."

I paused to wave at an acquaintance of mine, then turned back to him and said, "I think it's my favorite too. It's so much more me than Mardi Gras."

"Mardi Gras contains too many people in too small of a space. Jazz Fest is more spread out."

"Yeah, and whereas Mardi Gras brings out the worst in some people, Jazz Fest seems to bring out the best."

Inside, I saw some girls dancing barefoot in the mud, and I realized that I, too, could dance barefoot in the mud. So I did. Why not?

Ethan just stood off on the sidelines, looking at me as if I were some wondrous creature who had just landed from another planet. When I came back over to him, he asked, "So what did it feel like?"

"I liked it so much that from this point forward I think I'll try to dance barefoot in the mud as often as possible."

"Yes! That can be your Indian name: She who dances in the mud."

At one of the craft booths, they were selling some floral head crowns. Ethan bought me one, saying, "If anyone should wear one of these, it's you." I put it on, and he said, "You look like a princess."

I laughed and said, "Princess of the Mud." But I did actually feel like a princess around him. It was almost as if he were an alchemist, and in his presence, all my flaws and imperfections were transformed into something beautiful and whole and perfect. Although I wasn't all that attracted to him, I was attracted to myself when I was around him.

I got a water bottle, rinsed off, and put my sandals back on before heading over to the stage where our blues band was playing that afternoon. Erica, Katie, and Dana were already there, sitting on a big speaker. I climbed up to join them, and Ethan took our picture.

They were all staring at him—and especially at us—as we walked off afterward because it was the first time they had ever seen me with any guy besides bad boy Michael. Ethan didn't notice, but I did.

Oh well, I didn't care if we were the big news; I was having an excellent time. The whole day was splendid, up until the end when I accidentally sprained my ankle. I'm not sure how exactly—although I remember it did involve flying, leaping, and jumping.

There was a giant inflatable beer bottle set up as a display. I had seen some kids running, hurling into it, then flying off like superheroes. I thought it was a great idea, and my first few times doing it actually went pretty well. The last time? Not so good.

Anyway, Ethan managed to carry me all the way back to his car. I was very impressed by his strength and gallantry. To reward him, I stayed at his apartment for three whole days.

When he finally took me home, he actually carried me all the way upstairs to my apartment. Before leaving, he propped my foot up and brought me a drink and the telephone.

I called Erica first. Soon as she heard my voice, she said, "Good-looking, but not your type. Seriously—blonde hair?"

"You don't waste time with small talk."

"How can I? I've been waiting *days* to hear the details. Where've you been?"

"Ethan's—but it was unavoidable. I hurt my ankle, and he was my hero."

"Good. You deserve a hero . . . . So what's his apartment like? No—let me guess: a closet full of polo shirts and khaki pants, starched fresh from the cleaners."

I laughed. "You're always good at reading people. And yes, his place looks like the model apartment that they show prospective tenants."

"Well at least he's a pretty shoulder to cry on after all Michael put you through."

I called Josie next and told her, "I was tempted to stay at his place longer since my apartment is on the third floor; however, I have a good fling going with him, and I don't want to ruin it by either getting sick of him or falling in love—if that could even happen."

"Do you think it might?"

"Not really. I think of him more as a friend than a lover. He's a good listener, a good cook, and, incidentally, a good driver."

"A good driver?"

"Yeah. Usually I get nervous riding in people's cars, but with Ethan I enjoy just riding around with him because he drives so smoothly, responsibly, and confidently. I think that's the main reason I'm dating him—because he's safe."

Not only was Ethan safe, he was reliable too. He stopped by daily to bring me food. And when I went back to work, he came and picked me up and drove me there a few nights.

Then, fortunately, he went out of town for two weeks, which gave us a little break from all that coziness. When he came back, we resumed dating, but not every day.

With some people, an absence of that long or even much longer, is nothing; they just pick up where they left off, as if no time had passed. It wasn't like that with Ethan. After two weeks apart, it felt like starting over again. There was nothing unpleasant or uncomfortable about it. We just didn't have anything deep or intense between us. At least I didn't feel as if we did.

Ethan may have. He was still there at my beck and call and seemed to adore me. Whenever I'd get scared at night, or just didn't feel like being alone, I could call him at any time, and he would come pick me up and take me back to his place and wait on me hand and foot.

I told him, "I can conquer anything in the daytime. It's at nighttime that I get lonely, or scared, or terrified, whatever. They say escapism is not the answer, and I know it's probably not, but it works as a temporary solution."

He looked at me directly and said, "If I'm just a temporary solution, I'm okay with that. But I'm available for long-term too. I'll be here as long as you want me to be."

Poor Ethan. We were basically compatible, but there was no real charismatic passion . . . not like I was accustomed to anyway. I had the feeling that I could marry him and spend the rest of my life with him comfortably and peacefully—or never see him again. Either way would be okay. It didn't really matter.

Still, maybe he was what I wanted or needed—or was supposed to want. I didn't know. Was it possible that what I wanted, and what I was supposed to want, were two different things? Was it possible to change what I wanted, or want what I had, or was there another possibility?

24

Visit from an Old Friend

One morning soon after that, the phone woke me up. It was Bianca: "Wake up, Sam! My schedule changed, and I'm here about a week earlier than I planned."

"Oh wow. I knew you were coming soon. I just didn't realize *soon* was today."

"Yet here I am! I tried to call and let you know, but I couldn't get a hold of you. When are you going to get a cell phone?"

"Hey—I don't want to fry my brain cells."

"Well you could at least get voice mail. Anyway, I can just stay for the day because I have an interview in Dallas tomorrow. Do you already have plans?"

"Nope. You're in luck. I'm off work today and totally free. Come on over."

When she arrived, I gave her a tour of my apartment, which, of course, didn't take very long. She liked the way I had painted the furniture. "You always like to make your surroundings more colorful, Sam."

"You wanna see colorful surroundings? Come on and I'll give you a tour of the Quarter."

"That sounds great! Are you hungry? I'll take you out to eat. I'll feed you whatever you want."

We went to Napoleon House so she could have some local flavor. I ate the gumbo and she ate the jambalaya. The Beethoven playing in the background was soothing and conducive to conversation.

Afterward, I took her by The Blue. Not so conducive. Roger seated us and told Jennifer to get us whatever we wanted. It was loud and didn't really seem to be Bianca's scene, so we only stayed for one drink.

We left there and headed over to Café du Monde. We got two coffees to go, then went up the steps of the Washington Artillery Park river overlook, across from Jackson Square, and sat on a bench.

"Sam, this view is incredible! Most cities look alike, but not this one. This is totally unique."

"That's what I like about it. Sensory overload of colors, sights, sounds, smells, flavors, and I like to taste them all."

She looked at me and smiled. "Yes, it's appropriate for you. I liked uptown, but the French Quarter is a little too dark and dusty for me. I don't know how you can work at that blues club. The dust hanging off everything has a life of its own."

"For us, the dust is just part of it. Every cobweb has a story to tell and has just as much right to be there as we do. Not that we're spider lovers or anything, it's just the French Quarter way to leave things as they are."

"Maybe you do belong here after all."

"Wanna walk around a little more? You might still feel the magic."

"Sure. I have a little more time before I have to go."

We ran into Michael as we were heading back to her car and visited with him for a few minutes.

After he walked off, Bianca said, "So that's the man who stole your heart and married you to the French Quarter?"

"The French Quarter seduced me all by itself. And Michael didn't steal my heart, he just borrowed it for a little while . . . might have trampled on it a little bit too. I don't know. I haven't gotten it back completely yet."

"I don't see all the attention about him. Granted, he is good-looking, in an artistic kind of way."

"Well, you haven't slept with him yet, but I could probably arrange it."

"He's that bad, huh?"

"Or that good, depending on who you ask."

"What a tramp."

"The man believes in free love. I'm gonna have to figure out how to get away from him completely."

"I thought y'all broke up."

"Yeah, but we still hook up."

"Oh . . . ."

"Yeah . . . ."

I walked her to her car, and we said our big goodbye. It was great seeing her, and we'd had a very pleasant visit; however, as soon as she left, I felt insecure, depressed, and had that gaping-hole feeling inside of me that I sometimes get.

I bought a quart of beer at the deli, headed over to the river, and sat on an empty wooden bench near the end of the Moonwalk. I was hoping my bench would stay empty, but it didn't. A conservatively dressed couple sat down next to me. I nodded acknowledgment to them, pulled out my notebook, and started writing.

Three young boys, each about ten years old, kept racing by on their bikes. The woman next to me said, "I bet their mother doesn't even know where they are."

I looked over at her slowly, raised an eyebrow, and said, "Y'all must not be from around here."

The man said, "Actually we're not. We're visiting from Texas. By the way, do you know why they call this the Moonwalk?"

"They named it after a Mayor, Mayor Moon Landrieu."

"And how far down is the part they call the Moonwalk?"

"Originally it was this part here with the wooden benches, near Jackson Square, but now I think some people call it that the whole way down."

"Oh thanks! We had asked a couple of people, but no one seemed to know."

"You're welcome."

The woman said, "Hey, would you like to come to dinner with us tonight? We always like to visit with the real locals whenever we go on vacation. We'll take you out to Galatoire's. We hear it's really nice there."

"Thanks, but I already have plans." I resumed writing in my notebook.

At that point, some woman making her way down the walk yelled, "Fuckin' right! Lookin' at me crazy in the face! Look somewhere else, you crazy-ass bitch! Mother Fucker! Don't fuck with me! I saw you lookin' at me."

I made sure I didn't look up at all as she got near or passed. She pivoted and turned around going back. The couple on the bench next to me looked over. I told them nonchalantly, "Yeah, I saw her last night on Bourbon Street acting the same way, yelling the same stuff. Just try to avoid eye contact with her."

I told them bye, then headed over to the newer, shinier Riverwalk, where the trees look like weeping willows but they're really not. At least I don't think they are; it's not as if I'm a tree expert or anything.

A pathetic looking homeless woman shuffled past me, saying, "I ain't eaten in two days. Can you gimme a dollar or sump'n?" I told her I didn't have any money, which, sadly, was true.

I sat down on one of the steps, right past the Riverboat and started working on a poem. A precious little dark-haired boy, about two years old, walked right next to me, looked at me, then hopped down the stairs one at a time, like a bunny. His mother came running after him. She looked at me and said, "He has no fear; I have to have it for him."

I smiled and said, "What a beautiful thing to have no fear."

Some guy on a cell phone kept looking over at me while he was talking. After he hung up, he walked over and asked, "You're Michael's girlfriend, aren't you?"

I hesitated a moment, then told him, "Yes," because I didn't want him to think I was available.

He told me "Oh well, take it easy then," and moved on. That was the part about being single that sucked—I'd have to remember how to turn guys down that I had absolutely no interest in.

An older couple, probably in their eighties, sat down on a bench near me. The man pulled out a clarinet and began to play. The music was so beautiful and soothing that I would've liked to have stayed and listened for hours; however, I had to head home to get ready for work.

I got up and took one last look at the Mississippi. The river was the touchstone for the Quarter, flowing past all the things that changed, as well as all the things that didn't. Different water droplets, same river.

I walked past Jax Brewery, then turned left on St. Peter's and walked through Jackson Square. It was starting to get dark, and an old man sitting on a bench told me, "Goodnight, sister." I smiled and told him, "Goodnight."

I turned right on Chartres and sat down on a bench for a minute to rest, right in front of the cathedral. The schizophrenic man I had seen laying on the floor in the bookstore one night came walking by. He stopped in front of me, pointed over to the cathedral, and asked, "Is *this* God? *This* recipe? This set of instructions that I'm supposed to follow exactly? Or is *that* recipe? Or the other? Whose potato salad is He?"

I shrugged and told him, "I don't know."

He continued, "He? She? It? Us? Who decided that this unlimited Being could be contained in a pronoun?" He laughed and said, "Who indeed? *I* can hardly be contained in a pronoun." Then he walked off.

I had been pondering what it would have been like if I had stayed in school and graduated and was now taking that road trip with Bianca. For a moment, I connected with that alternate person that I would have been if I had stayed on that path.

But if I had done that, I wouldn't have had these influences. I wouldn't be this person, not exactly. I wasn't sure that I wanted to be this person living this life; however, I felt confident that I was heading in the direction of the person I wanted to be. I was meandering there persistently, if sometimes slowly.

When I got home, I ate some leftover rice and vegetables, and laughed when I remembered that I could've had dinner at Galatoire's if I had wanted to.

Later, as I headed in to work, I felt as if I were ready for some things to be different, but I just wasn't sure I was ready to do anything about it yet. When I got there, I was in the mood to talk to Erica, but she was off that night.

I tried to express my feelings to Jennifer, telling her, "I don't have the mentality of a lazy person, but the results have been the same. I just haven't enjoyed it as much."

She laughed and said, "Well have another drink and it won't bother you. That's what I do. When you're drunk, it doesn't seem that awful. But when you're sober, it can get really depressing."

I remembered that day I had decided to drop out of the ordinary and move into the French Quarter. I wasn't living a boring conventional life now; however, I had fallen into a pool of stagnation. I had received signs that I was ready to move on to something else; however, I'd had no significant catalyst that had forced me to move on yet.

Later that night, there was some type of catalyst. A blonde-haired woman came into the club, dancing along to the music. A black man followed closely along behind her, slipped his arm around her waist, and started dancing with her.

Instantaneously, Roger was there. He slammed the man's head to the ground and held him motionless in some martial arts hold for probably five minutes—seemed like an hour—while waiting for the cops. When they finally arrived, Roger reluctantly released his death grip, and the man slowly got up, obviously in pain. The cops talked to him for a few minutes and to the woman, then let them go.

After the cops left, Roger came over to me and said lamely, "Turns out the woman was the man's wife. How was I supposed to know that?"

I looked him straight in the eye and said, "That wasn't right what you did."

He looked like he was going to say something, thought better of it, and skulked off. Maybe even he realized that he had crossed the line. I had seen him get physically violent over anger on several occasions; however, I had never seen him get physically violent over blind prejudice.

I had one of those, "What am I still doing here?" moments and couldn't come up with an answer.

A few of us dragged ourselves over to Nugent's after work. When we got there, I sat down next to a cop at the bar. He was one of the cops who had come in The Blue earlier to sort out Roger's mess.

I asked him, "So, did anything exciting happen tonight other than the brutalization of a poor man just trying to dance with his wife?"

He shook his head and said, "I know; that was ridiculous. But no, other than that, it was a very boring night."

"What about last night? I saw a couple of ambulances, saw some cops trotting by on horses, saw people running."

"Uh, that's what I call a boring night, just routine stuff. There weren't any murders, nobody killed. Boring."

"So if you call that boring, what's an exciting night?"

"Blood and guts."

"And when's the last time you had something like that?"

"Last week—out at the St. Thomas projects. Guy shot eight times. Lot of blood, lot of guts."

"And I thought my job was tough. It sounds to me like a boring night is a good thing."

"Yes, it is. Yes, it is."

Just then, Erica came in. I wanted to talk to her about the Roger stuff; however, she had just broken up with Jake, so that obviously took precedence.

She was slightly put out, but not too upset. "He called and asked what I wanted to do on our night off. I was about to try to think of something, but then I just told him, 'Let's not do this anymore, Jake. Nothing personal, we'll keep it all friendly, but we're taking our time heading nowhere, so let's just end it now and move on.'"

"Wow! How'd he take it?"

"I think he was hoping to get lucky tonight, but other than that, he seemed to take it well. We just talked for a few more minutes, then said goodbye and hung up."

"That's good. Nice and quick. You were smart enough to get out before all the melodrama."

"Maybe I learned from your mistakes after all."

"Hey, don't judge love by my history. You have to write your own story. I just recommend not living together prematurely. Above and beyond that, you should probably take all love advice from Guru Seth."

She smiled and asked, "How was work tonight?"

After I told her about it, she said, "No way! I can't believe Roger did that. Well, I can almost believe it—I just didn't know he'd go that far."

"I know. That's the part that's hard to believe. I knew he had it in him; I just didn't know it would come out of him that aggressively—and obviously. Do you want another drink?"

"Sure."

I ordered another round, then continued, "Since I have to see Roger and deal with him regularly, I've tried to believe in his goodness and have tried to look for and appreciate good things about him."

"Good luck with that."

"Seriously. I believe everybody has good in them, but they don't always act that way. So when they're not acting that way, we're just not seeing the good, but I can still believe it's there. Kind of like the sun's always there, but we can't always see it, especially if there are clouds in the way."

"Now we've got Guru Seth and Guru Samantha."

"Laugh if you want to, but that's what I believe—or try to anyway. When Roger does something like he did tonight, it sort of shatters my whole vision . . . or upsets it anyway."

"It is upsetting, but you'll get over it, Samantha. You know why? Because you want to. But Roger probably won't change." She took a sip of her drink and added, "You know what the worst part of Roger is? The fact that he has to live with himself."

"That's true. The people who disturb us are just a small part of our lives, but they have to deal with themselves 24-7."

We hung out a little longer then decided to walk home. As we rounded the corner onto Bourbon, two guys fell in stride behind us. The guy on the right yelled out, "Must be jam because jelly sure don't shake like that."

The one on the left added, "Yeah, I'd like to get my hands on some of that."

I turned around and said, "Please keep your comments to yourself."

"We'll give our comments to anyone we like!"

Erica turned around and said to one of them, "Look, I know you. You shouldn't be acting that way."

He said, "I didn't say it. He's the one talking. Don't be so sensitive. Besides, this is a free country. We can say whatever we want to say."

I told him, "If you're trying to pick up women, that's not the way to go about it."

He said, "Fuck you!"

The other one said, "Yeah, fuck you, bitch."

At that point, Erica and I ditched the walking idea and jumped in a cab on the corner. As we did so, one of them yelled, "Yeah, jump in a cab and take your asses home you two bitches. Don't have any business bein' out on the street this time o' night anyway if you're not offerin' anything."

As we rode home, Erica said, "Those are some cloudy boys, huh? Where's the sun now, Sam?"

I laughed and said, "Maybe it will roll back in after their booze wears off."

A little while later, as I closed my eyes to go to sleep, I suddenly had a very strange sense, like a word I couldn't quite remember, or a taste, but of what? I felt genderless . . . timeless. Some lyrics came into my head, and I got up and wrote them down.

Each group has their
Own ideal
What they want to see
When they look in the mirror
How they think they're
Supposed to feel
Who they think
They're supposed to be

But before we're born
And after we die
Do these labels
Really apply?
Man, Woman
Black, White,
Mother, Child
Christian, Jew
Take away my body
Look inside of me
Take away your body
And I'll look inside of you
Then tell me what is true
Tell me what is true

Culture and
Geography
What's that got
to do with me?
It tells me who I am
Or who I think I'm
supposed to be
But is it really me?
Is it really me?

25

My Jumping-Off Place

The next day, I rode the bus downtown to go to the bank. As soon as I got on, I realized that walking might have been better; the bus was hot and stuffy. The air conditioning needed some Freon or something. I was instantly assaulted with a thousand different scents and odors, mostly unpleasant: hairspray, perfume, cologne, etc.

At one of the stops, a guy got on the bus wearing a dog leash wrapped around his neck, looped through six CD's. He was bopping his head, dancing a little, and snapping his fingers. It looked like he was listening to music, but he wasn't. He caught some girl's eye and started trying to talk to her, but she quickly turned away.

There was also a lady picking her nose. I looked right at her and she looked right at me—looking right at her—and kept right on picking. Was she that oblivious to social convention?

I got off the bus and there it was—a dead bird. I always look at dead birds on the sidewalk. I don't know why I don't instantly look away. My eyes are chained to the scene until that last moment when I know I'm about to throw up; then I forcefully tear my eyes away. Maybe that's what I was still doing in New Orleans. Maybe I just hadn't reached that last moment yet.

That night as I was heading to work, some tourist guy started walking alongside me. He said, "You sure walk fast. Where are you going in such a hurry? Can I come with you?"

Without slowing my stride or even looking at him, I told him, "I'm not interested."

"What do you mean you're not interested?"

Just then, one of the local mugger thugs slid out of the shadows and authoritatively told him, "Look, the lady said she's not interested. Now beat it!"

The guy took off. I was a little unnerved by the whole thing, but I nodded acknowledgement to the thug and kept walking.

Okay maybe I had finally reached that last moment. Surely I had obtained full residency as a local—the mugger thug had stepped out to protect me! That's one thing I had discovered: for the most part, locals in the Quarter looked after one another. Still, I didn't think it would go that far.

When I got to work, I marched over to Roger and gave him my two-week notice. I'd stared at that dead bird long enough. It felt really great too. I suddenly felt lighter and freer and more energized.

I told Seth, "I just quit on a whim. I didn't plan this ahead of time. I have absolutely no idea what I'm going to do next, or where I'm going to go."

"Does that make you nervous?"

"No," I said smiling. "I like it. Things have started to suck lately, and for the first time in a long time, I'm really excited. I think that waking up not knowing what's going to happen that day is so much more stimulating than waking up feeling like every day is going to be exactly like the day before. Do you know what I mean?"

"Well you know *I* do, Samantha, but everybody wouldn't. Apparently, some people prefer to have a daily routine."

"Well maybe some people prefer the known monotony to the vastness of the unknown, but not me!"

He laughed and said, "Me neither. I'll probably be the next person here to turn in my two-week notice."

Erica was shocked that I was just quitting unexpectedly and hadn't discussed it with her at all in advance. Upon hearing the news, she marched over to me and asked, "Is there anything we can do to change your mind?"

"No. Sometimes you just get a gut feeling that you have to do something, and you gotta go with it. I do anyway. It's the same kind of gut feeling that brought me to New Orleans in the first place."

Katie overheard and said, "Just like Mary Poppins. The wind changed, so it was time for her to go. There was no talking her out of it."

Dana added, "You are kind of like Mary Poppins. Well, maybe a cross between her and Billie Holiday."

I smiled. "That's probably more like it."

Erica said, "Well I don't like it. I think you should stay."

We continued the conversation at Nugent's after work. Erica asked me, "Well what are you gonna do? I know Roger would let you cancel your two-week notice."

I laughed. "Forget it, darling. Not gonna happen."

She frowned, then said, "Well Josie would hire you, if you wanted."

"Yeah, but I wouldn't want to do that to her."

"But you're going to stay in the Quarter, right? You know you could get a job just about anywhere you want around here."

"Actually, I may not stay. I'm thinking about taking off for California."

"California! You've got to be kidding me! That's halfway across the world."

"Not quite." I reached over and held her hand. "Look, Erica, I'll be back. And you and I are like sisters, right? We'll always stay in touch."

She smiled sadly. "When are you leaving?"

As soon as my two-week notice is up. I'm almost at the end of my lease on my apartment too, so it works out perfectly. I was gonna renew, but now I won't."

"Do you know anyone in California?"

"No, but I didn't know anyone in New Orleans either when I moved here."

"Do you think you might stay out there?"

"No. New Orleans is my true home, but right now I feel like a discontented child living here. I just need a break for a few months. Who knows? Maybe I'll just go away for the summer and come back in the fall."

I said goodbye, then headed over to Josephine's, feeling confident that I had done the right thing. If I had given up college, at least for the time being, for some great adventure, and this great adventure was over, then it was time to move on to the next one. If I wasn't going back to a civilized life yet, then I at least better be doing something fabulous with my life! San Francisco just might be my next big thing.

Josie wasn't working, but Matt was there. I told him about my impending departure and said, "This entire time in New Orleans I felt as if I was here for a purpose, but I didn't know what it was."

"Do you know now?"

"Not sure. I used to think everything happened for a reason, and that eventually that reason would be revealed. Now, I'm no longer sure I believe that . . . . I may have just been wasting my time."

"I seriously doubt that."

"Yeah, me too. However, I don't think there's necessarily just one reason for anything. I think we take out of a situation whatever we want, positive or negative. Each experience has whatever meaning we give to it."

"So what do you think you've gotten out of this experience?"

"Well, for one thing, I've started writing a book. You know those reoccurring dreams I've had about New Orleans in the 1800's?"

"Yeah."

"Well I've started writing sort of a historical novel."

"I can't wait to read it. That sounds like a good enough reason for being here."

"Not just that though. There was another reason. This was my jumping-off place."

"Like off a cliff?"

"Yes, but into a clear blue lagoon, or down a waterfall into a deep river, or something amazing like that, where, afterward, nothing will ever be the same."

"Like a whole different world."

"Yeah, sort of like that. I'm still the same person, but I've let go of a lot of my preconceived notions of how I'm supposed to be, or how life is supposed to be, or how anything's supposed to be, really. Maybe there is no *supposed* to be. Maybe everything is just choice and consequence. And as it turns out, there are a lot more choices than I once realized. I feel like I can go anywhere I want to go and do anything I want to do."

"You've always been somewhat of a free spirit."

"Maybe we all are, but sometimes we just don't realize it."

Matt looked me for a moment, then said, "You know I've always loved you."

"I've always loved you too."

We hugged—one of those hugs where time seems to stand still—and it had nothing to do with passion and everything to do with comfort. I felt as if I had always known him.

I walked home along the river, and everything looked different. Everything was different. My life, up until New Orleans, had been a life of semi-ambitious conformity. I knew it never would be again, not unless I chose that anyway, which is different than conforming because you think you have no choice or because you don't even realizing that you are doing it.

Anyway, I still wasn't sure where my path would lead, but I knew that I would follow it.

When I told Ethan about my plans to leave, he said, "I'd never want to hold you back from anything you want to do, but if possible, I'd still like to spend whatever time I can with you until you leave."

I stroked his cheek and smiled at him. "I really appreciate the way you've treated me, Ethan. It's almost like this relationship has made up for other bad stuff in my life . . . . Crazy that I'm walking away, I know."

He just looked down and didn't say anything.

I tilted his chin up, looked in his eyes, and said, "I really hope someday you find the perfect woman, worthy of you. Because you are worthy. I don't know what it's taken to get you to this point, but you really are a good guy."

He just wasn't Michael. *Oh . . . Michael.* Soon after the incident with that red-haired woman in my apartment, he'd moved out completely, and we'd officially broken up. I say *officially* because we obviously did not make a clean break privately. There had been too many lies, too many things said and done that couldn't be taken back for me to stay with him publicly. Yet every time he rang my doorbell, I found it impossible not to go down and let him in. Thus, we continued seeing each other in private until the night before I left town.

I dated Ethan publicly, but Michael was my behind-the-scenes. I knew that leaving town was the only way I could let him go. And I had to let him go—I just had to.

He came over to my place the night before I left town. The gate downstairs was open, so he just came on up. When I opened the door of my apartment to let him in, he knelt before me and pleaded, "Don't go—or if you have to go, take me with you!"

"You must be joking, right?"

He stood up with tears in his eyes, took my hands in his, and said, "No. I'm very serious. Now that you've been with another man, I thought maybe you could understand. Because you still care for me, right? Do you understand how that works now?"

I guided him over to the couch and said, "That even though you slept with someone else it doesn't mean you love me any less?"

"Exactly. There's a part of you and me that always belongs together, regardless of what our other parts are doing."

Despite the tears that were beginning to form in my own eyes, I burst out laughing, which surprised Michael. He looked at me strangely.

I told him, "Oh, I just remembered the time I was sitting on this couch reading a book, and you just picked up my foot and started trimming my toenails without even saying anything first!"

"That's what I'm talking about! To me, it feels as if our two bodies are the same body, regardless of what they do when they're apart from one another."

"Well, be that as it may, I can't live the lifestyle of a musician's girlfriend anymore. Not right now anyway. I have to be my own person, and for some reason I can't do that with you."

"Why is that?"

"Because when I'm with you, it *is* like I'm yours. But you're not mine. You're yours too. We're both yours."

He got a thoughtful look on his face and said, "I never knew you felt that way. I don't feel that way, baby." He reached for my hand, raised one eyebrow and said, "I really *do* want to come with you."

"But you know I have to go alone, right?"

"You're not scared to go alone?"

"No. I don't feel as if I'm afraid of anything right now."

"Will you come back to me?"

I grinned and said, "I still haven't learned how to read the future yet. All I've learned to do is create my present."

"Well that's a major accomplishment. Still, I wish I was a part of it."

He suddenly stood up and said, "Oh well, if you won't take me with you, I'm taking you with me." He picked me up and carried me to the door.

I was laughing and telling him to put me down. He did, then said, "I have to go to work now, but if you reconsider, come get me. I'll leave right in the middle of my gig and follow you wherever you want to go. I'll follow you to the ends of the earth if you let me."

After he left, I curled up on the couch and took a nap. Almost instantly, I dreamed that I was back in 19th century New Orleans again. I was running down a street, almost skipping. So happy and excited—I was on my way to meet the man I loved.

I heard footsteps coming from behind. I laughed, thinking that was going to be him, then turned around and froze.

It wasn't him. It was a man with blonde hair. I knew him. And I could tell instantly that he was in one of his rages.

Just then, my lover called to me—in despair. I looked around, and saw him being led off by some other men. I knew right then that I would never see him again. I screamed, "NO!" with every cell in my body, and sank to the ground.

The blonde-haired man approached and stood over me, his face still in a rage, his body ready to explode. I didn't care; I just stayed there. All I could think about was my man. He was gone . . . .

Just then, I woke up from the dream and laid there, still feeling it all.

Was that man I had been trying to go meet in my dream Michael? The man that was being led off? *Michael, my sweet love.* Sorry darling, but this time, it just wasn't working out either . . . . Not right now anyway. Some tears rolled down my cheeks. I wiped them away, then got up and continued packing to leave.

When I was all finished, I went and sat out on the roof to take one last look around at all the French Quarter rooftops. *Goodbye New Orleans. Goodbye Michael . . . for now anyway.*

New Orleans was the only place that had ever truly felt like home to me, and I had a feeling it would be a while—if ever—before I found someplace else that made me feel the same way. But I was ready to start looking.

Epilogue

I have yet to see Michael again in person, but he still shows up in a dream every once in a while. Never anything romantic though. We just get together and visit sometimes, somewhere in our subconscious—a meeting of our minds or souls or whatever. That may be a better, safer place for us to connect than actual physical reality. He was lousy as a boyfriend, and sometimes even as a human being, but somewhere deep inside of him was a little something beautiful.

Josie and I wrote back and forth for a while. Then, we didn't. Recently, I tried to call Josephine's, but it's no longer there. Maybe Josie made it to Paris. I like to think so. That's where I picture her anyway.

Matt and I emailed poems back and forth a few times, but it turned out that our relationship was lost without ambiance, and emailing each other didn't have the same charismatic energy that our impromptu get-togethers at Josephine's had had, so that fizzled out as well.

I stayed in touch with some of my other friends from New Orleans for a little while, but we finally lost touch. Our addresses have all changed too many times since then. That's one bad thing about women changing their names when they get married: It makes it very difficult to find old friends.

I still have that picture of Erica, Katie, Dana and me at Jazz Fest. I have no idea where they are now, or what they're up to, but in that picture, the four of us are always sitting there smiling. We might have been happy too.

It's strange, isn't it, how some people can be such a part of your microcosm for a certain period of time in your life . . . then nothing. We went our separate ways, and our individual worlds no longer intersect, not directly anyway. I wonder, sometimes, when I think of one of them, if they are, at that moment, thinking of me.

Funny how I once thought I would never be able to leave New Orleans. Since then, I have lived in eight different cities and traveled through seventeen different countries. But that's another story . . . .

And did I ever go back to New Orleans? No. But I'm about to . . . .

Lagniappe

The literal translation of Lagniappe is "a little something extra."

It can mean anything from an extra bonus item thrown in with your order from the bakery to a supplemental section of the newspaper (or in this case, a book).

If you have come to the end of this novel and it has left you wanting more, this section is here to offer *a little something extra*. Just when you thought you'd reached the end of the story, *lagniappe* keeps it moving along.

It's only fitting because the French Quarter is a never ending story; *Life in the French Quarter* is a story within a story. The city is full of stories. New Orleans is a place where stories begin.

So sit back, relax, and let the story roll on. As the locals say, "L'aissez le bon temps roulez." (Let the good times roll.)

How My Book Came to Be . . .

When I went to Loyola, my friends and I used to sit around and take turns reading different parts of favorite books out loud. At the time, there weren't any slice of life novels about contemporary New Orleans, at least none that I was aware of. Toni Morrison said, "If there's a book you really want to read but it hasn't been written yet, then you must write it." And that's exactly what I set out to do.

I moved into the French Quarter with the intention of writing a book about it. I did work in a blues bar, and in my free time, I used to sit in bars and write on bev naps or coasters, or I'd hang out in Jackson Square or the Moonwalk. I wrote down EVERYTHING! Everything I saw, everything I heard, everything I did. Everything.

Then, about once a week, I'd stay home and put all my different scraps into a big notebook. I filled up several of those notebooks.

Years later, I pulled them out and started trying to do something with them. My first draft (a million drafts ago!) was nonfiction, but it didn't make sense. Real life often doesn't make sense. It was illogical, inconsistent, didn't have any flow, and none of the loose ends tied up neatly.

So I transformed it into fiction. Picasso said, "Art is the lie that tells the truth." I feel that this piece of fiction gives a more accurate portrayal of what the French Quarter is actually like than my initial journals did.

Hope you've enjoyed reading it as much as I enjoyed researching and writing it!

Love,
Andrea

Select Excerpts

"The **French Quarter** is its own country. There are a lot of people who've grown up here and never left—probably never will leave either unless they're forced out at gunpoint—maybe not even then. There are also people who came here from other places, maybe just to visit even, but then they stayed. There's something about this place." (18)

I left there and went on to the **French Market**. Even though there were some touristy things there, it had actually been a market since the 1800's, maybe even earlier than that, and was originally just a place for the locals to do their shopping.

That's what it was for me. If I wanted an avocado, or a cucumber, or a Halloween pumpkin, or a Christmas tree (or a prescription for some disturbing dreams), that's where I went. Of course if a tourist wanted gourmet sauces, or alligator on a stick, or an eel skin wallet, or some tee shirts, they could get those things there too.

There was a sign at the entrance that said: "Quality is like buying oats. If you want good clean oats, you must pay a fair price. If, however, you are satisfied with oats after they have already passed through the horse, well then, they are a little cheaper." It was appropriate for the French Market too because you could find things from both ends there. (173-174)

The next thing I do remember is the **King Cake**. Hidden inside those things somewhere beneath the purple, green, and gold sugar is a plastic baby, and whoever gets it is supposed to host the next party or buy the next cake or whatever.

Anyway, I guess I had gotten one of those little miniature King Cakes at the deli. Apparently, I started eating it and—hey! I got the baby! That's what I remember: the icky feeling of biting into the plastic baby brought me back to conscious awareness of my environment for a few moments. Then I must have passed out. (148)

I got up and took one last look at the **Mississippi**. The river was the touchstone for the Quarter, flowing past all the things that changed, as well as all the things that didn't. Different water droplets, same river. (187)

Characters

Bianca ~ Samantha's former college roommate.

Dana ~ bartender at The Blue. "She was gorgeous and got a lot of attention for that, but she wasn't sweet, and she wasn't easy. She could out-drink and out-curse any man, and make him regret it if he didn't treat her with the respect, dignity, and admiration she deserved." (107)

Danny ~ the bass player at The Blue. He and Katie live together.

Erica ~ cocktail waitress at The Blue. "We've got a pretty good deal here, and as long as we show up and do our work, the managers don't harass us over petty matters, such as drinking on the job." (15)

Ethan ~ attorney. "It was almost as if he were an alchemist, and in his presence, all my flaws and imperfections were transformed into something beautiful and whole and perfect. Although I wasn't all that attracted to him, I was attracted to myself when I was around him." (180)

Jennifer ~ cocktail waitress at The Blue. "Well have another drink and it won't bother you. That's what I do. When you're drunk, it doesn't seem that awful. But when you're sober, it can get really depressing." (188)

Josie ~ Bartender and owner of Josephine's. "She had long black hair, which she was wearing in two long braids, and she looked sort of like a medieval princess." (19)

Katie ~ bartender at The Blue. ". . . to her, the French Quarter scene is both normal and innocent." (34)

Matt ~ poet. "His hair was long and brown and looked as if he hadn't brushed it in a long time. He looked clean though; he actually smelled like soap. He was ten or twenty years older than me and had sort of a timeless face." (68)

Michael ~ guitar player. "His roommate situation wasn't working out, so at first I thought that his staying with me was just a temporary thing, even as I saw more of his belongings gradually making their way over to my place. I thought it would be better if we each had our own space and just spent as much time together as we wanted to— even if it was all the time." (18, 19)

Roger ~ manager at The Blue. "He would lumber over to potential customers, chest puffing out, and ask them if they wanted a table as if he were challenging them with, 'What did you say about my mother!' Then, as he went to seat them, he would do a little move where it looked like he was trying to get his underwear out of his butt without using his hands. I think that was part of his tough guy walk. And it wasn't just an act either. He was prepared to follow through on it—and often did." (136)

Samantha ~ main character. "I'm always changing. I don't want to be restricted by something I thought I was yesterday." (52) "I'm not looking for a guru. I'm just trying to find my own path." (53)

Seth ~ bartender at The Blue. "Well everyone has the freedom to choose whatever works for them. The key is this: whenever something no longer works for you, find something else that does. Keep living. Keep loving." (108)

Tony ~ Laundromat employee. "He was always flitting around, dancing, twirling, singing, 'I am so beautiful,' as well as tunes from various Broadway and off-Broadway productions." (30)

Index

www.LifeInTheFrenchQuarter.com

www.facebook.com/LifeInTheFrenchQuarter

www.myspace.com/LifeInTheFrenchQuarter